JUSTIN

CW00802776

PIRATE
ACADEMY

BOOK TWO:
MISSING AT SEA

with illustrations
by Teo Skaffa

uclanpublishing

PRAISE FOR PIRATE ACADEMY

"It's another gem – carefully crafted, compelling characters and all sorts of intrigue. The Academy already has enough to recommend it, filled as it is with swashbuckling legends and satisfying turns and tussles along the way. But the tale of friendship and family ties it all together in a nifty nautical knot."
Guy Bass

"A swashbuckling pirate school adventure with loyalty and friendship at its core."
Janine Beacham

"Set in a brilliant nautical world full of danger and daring, PIRATE ACADEMY: NEW KID ON DECK had me racing through the pages to find out what would happen next!"
Jennifer Bell

"A storming success! Justin is at the top of his game with this funny, thrilling and full-on high-seas adventure."
Chris Bradford

"All the rip-roaring adventure you would expect from a Justin Somper book. Pirates done right! I love this world."
Eoin Colfer

"A gloriously action-packed adventure, full of characters you really care about."
Cressida Cowell

"Such a fun adventure story that made me want to be a pirate! Written with heart and humour by one of the best in the business."
Laura Dockrill

"With characters you'll want as your best friends forever, this is a glorious thrill of a salty saga – spine tingling, fast moving, totally unputdownable!"
Vivian French

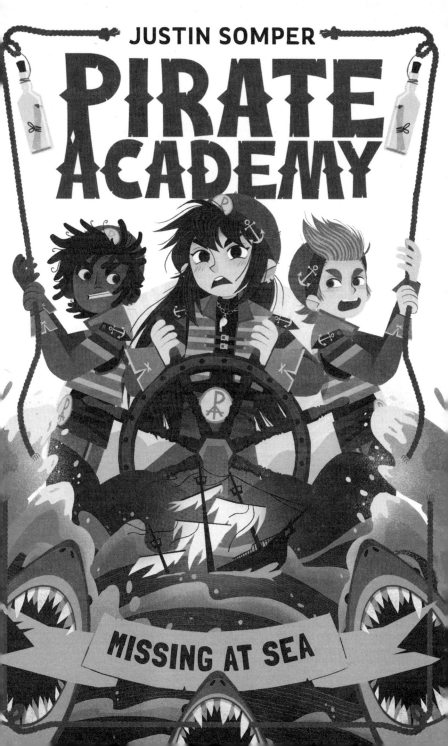

Pirate Academy: Missing At Sea is a uclanpublishing book

First published in Great Britain in 2024 by uclanpublishing
University of Central Lancashire
Preston, PR1 2HE, UK

Text copyright © Justin Somper 2024
Cover artwork © Teo Skaffa 2024

978-1-916747-03-6

1 3 5 7 9 10 8 6 4 2

Set in 11.5/17pt Kingfisher by Amy Cooper

A CIP catalogue record for this book is available from the British Library.

Printed and bound in Great Britain by Clays Ltd, Elcograf S.p.A.

for David Amstel and Andrew Davidson,
two of the best friends a boy could ask for –
in smooth or rough weather.

THE STORY SO FAR . . .

It is the year 2507. The world's oceans are under the control of the Pirate Federation.

Jasmine Peacock and Jacoby Blunt are two of the fifteen students in Barracuda Class at Pirate Academy, Coral Sea Province. Here, the children of the ocean's fiercest pirate families are being trained by the world's greatest captains. On Captains' Evening, Jacoby gets a horrendous report and is warned he must do better. For Jasmine, it's even worse – her parents fail to show up for Captains' Evening and are declared 'missing at sea'.

That very night, a new student, the mysterious Neo Splice, arrives at the Academy harbour. The Barracudas are a tight-knit unit and, to begin with, Neo has a bit of a bumpy ride joining the class. But the Barracudas instantly rally round Neo when he shares a massive secret with them. 'Neo Splice' is his new identity. He was born Ned Darkwater, only son of legendary pirate Captain Doll Darkwater. Neo's mum was killed on her ship by a dangerous new organisation called the League of True Pirates that plans to seize control of the oceans.

The ruthless members of LOT P have unfinished business with Neo and have followed him to Pirate Academy. During Sailing Class, they kidnap Neo, along with his classmate Priya. The Headcaptain launches a bold rescue mission. The LOT P crew puts up a strong fight. Neo is rescued but Priya reveals that she is now a member of LOT P and plans to stay with them.

As the LOT P crew is forced to surrender, Jasmine is shocked to discover that her uncle, Noah Ripley, is one of the ringleaders of the rebel organisation. Before Ripley is taken away to prison, she begs him for news of her parents. But, after trying to recruit Jasmine herself, he falls silent.

Back at Pirate Academy, Neo reveals to Jacoby that they are half-brothers. Jacoby is thrilled at this news, but they agree to keep it their secret for now.

Meanwhile, Jasmine is delivered a very special music box belonging to her mother, Parker Ripley Peacock. On the back of the box is a coded message, telling Jasmine that her parents are safe and will be in touch soon.

We pick up the story, four weeks later, at Pirate Academy . . .

CHAPTER 1
HIDE AND SEEK

He was making himself as small as possible. This wasn't easy, given how tall he had grown recently and how cramped the space was that he was hiding in. And he was making himself as quiet as a mouse – in fact *quieter*, he realised, as he watched a small furry creature emerge from the gloom and scurry excitedly towards his face. Silently, the boy drew his finger to his lips to tell the mouse to shush. But, whilst his sign might be recognised all over the world by humans, he wasn't sure if it would be understood by a rodent.

The boy was still reeling from the sight of his mother, sprawled on the bed in her cabin. *This* cabin. She lay only a few feet from him. Utterly still.

Her skin had been as cold as winter water to his touch. There was so much blood on the bedclothes, pooling out from where her heart still lay, though it was no longer beating. His own heart raced wildly. He could feel it and he could hear it, thumping heavily against his ribcage. In the confined space, the noise seemed louder, echoing around him. He was sure it was going to give away his hiding place, reveal his presence to the intruders – the evil people who had arrived in the night, boarded this ship and, with icy efficiency, killed his mother.

Dead. Murdered. The words were so strange in his head. He knew their meaning, of course, but it felt impossible to apply them to his own mother. The woman who had raised him these eleven years alone – who had taught him how to sail ships and navigate by starlight, to wield swords and crossbows almost as masterfully as she could. His mother, who had schooled him in how to grade diamonds and gold and how to quickly spot a real da Vinci from a fake. His mother, with whom he had eaten supper just a few hours earlier, out on the upper deck. They had laughed together, as the sun sank behind their sails, talking about this and that and nothing at all. The thought that he would never hear her throaty laugh again was already hard to bear.

Maybe he should just give himself up and allow them to take him too. It would likely be a quick death and it would take away this terrible fear, swelling in his belly like a demon. He knew they were getting closer.

He could hear footsteps and voices. It was only a matter of time. Their swords were thirsty again.

Now there came a knocking. Muffled at first, then clearer and louder. They must be here inside his mother's cabin, right in front of the cupboard he had hurled himself into. He froze, trying to think himself even smaller, even quieter. He noticed that the mouse had gone away, presumably bored by this game of sleeping pirates.

The knocking came again. Now he not only heard it but felt it ricochet through his body. It was as if they were already beating the living daylights out of him. His eyes were already closed but now he squeezed them even more tightly shut. As if that would protect him. The knocking grew louder, closer.

"Neo! Neo, are you there? Are you awake?"

He opened his eyes with a start.

He had been dreaming. He wasn't on the ship, *Death and the Maiden*, which he had called home for the best part of his life. He was here in his landlocked cabin at Pirate Academy. His body was tightly folded but he wasn't in the confines of a cupboard – he was simply twisted in the sheets of his bunk. He was no longer the boy called Ned Darkwater. He was . . .

"Neo! I can hear you in there! Let me in!"

He swung his legs over the bunk. He took a deep breath in and out of his belly, letting go of the nightmare, allowing his eyes to drink in the familiar surroundings of his room. The knocking came again.

"I'm coming!" he called out, padding over to the door and opening it.

"Have you seen the time?" Jacoby asked him, tapping his watch. "We're going to be late." Then his expression and voice changed. "Are you OK? You don't look OK."

Neo attempted a smile. "I'm . . . all right. I was just really deep in sleep, I guess."

Jacoby studied his face carefully. It reminded Neo of being examined by a doctor. Seeing that Jacoby was dressed in his aqua-coloured tracksuit pulled Neo's own thoughts into sharp focus. His new friend, who was also his secret brother, had – as usual – come to collect him for the 5k run which signalled the start of each new day for Barracuda Class.

"How late are we?" Neo asked.

"We need to be at Swashbuckle Hill in precisely nine minutes," Jacoby informed him, stepping into Neo's cabin. "Or we'll be doing hundreds of press-ups. And you *know* how I feel about press-ups!"

Neo nodded, already striding towards the bathroom.

Now Jacoby was here, the day was starting to feel more normal.

"You could miss brushing your teeth just this once," Jacoby said.

Neo shook his head. "Never neglect your personal hygiene," he said, popping his toothbrush in his mouth. He disappeared into the bathroom and completed a basic wash routine in under two minutes. Stepping back out again, satisfied he was smelling fresh, he quickly changed into his own aqua tracksuit and running shoes. Meanwhile, Jacoby anxiously watched the other Academy students through the window. His legs jiggled as they always did when he was tense.

"OK," Jacoby said. "We have five and a half minutes now. Can we do it?"

Neo grinned, his freshly polished teeth gleaming at his brother. "Never underestimate a Barracuda!"

CHAPTER 2
OCEANS BOUND

The school grounds were a riot of colour as students from eight year groups jogged through the lush gardens, each class wearing different coloured running gear. The older students ran 10k at the start of each day, whilst those in Crab, Squid and Barracuda Class ran 5k.

"You guys cut it fine this morning," Jasmine said to Jacoby and Neo as they jogged along side by side. "What happened?"

"I overslept!" Jacoby cried, speeding up as if he might be trying to run ahead of her.

Jasmine effortlessly increased her own pace so she was just ahead of the boys.

"You overslept?!" she exclaimed. "On today of all days!"

"I don't know what you're talking about," Jacoby said but, as their eyes met, she caught the grin spreading across his face. Jasmine and Jacoby had been great friends for five years and she was expert at reading his moods. "All right," he said. "Maybe I *do* know what you're talking about."

Having all speeded up, Jasmine, Jacoby and Neo had now caught up with Cosmo and Ocean, who gladly parted ways to give the others space to run alongside them. They had reached the base of Swashbuckle Hill and were now jogging alongside the sunlit harbour waters.

"So, Jacoby," Cosmo said, with a mischievous grin. "How do you rate your chances today?"

"I don't know what you're talking about," Jacoby said again.

"Argh!" Jasmine cried out. She glanced past Jacoby to exchange a knowing look with her roommate Ocean.

Cosmo turned to Neo. "Jacoby has been waiting for this moment – *dreaming* of this moment – from the day he first climbed up Swashbuckle Hill in his little knee-socks and sandals!"

"You're talking about Oceans Bound weekend, right?" Neo said.

"Correct!" Cosmo boomed. "Everyone knows that Oceans Bound is the true beginning of your life as a pirate." He called to Jacoby over Neo's head. "Admit it, Blunt, you've been obsessing about this weekend for years!"

"To be fair," Ocean cut in, "we all have. There's no getting away from it. Oceans Bound weekend *is* a Really Big Deal."

"I don't totally understand why," Neo said.

"That's because you only joined Barracuda Class a month ago," Cosmo said. "No offence intended."

"None taken," Neo replied. Jasmine was pleased to see how, after his first bumpy days, Neo had been fully welcomed into the tight-knit fold of the Barracudas. "Can you explain it to me?" Neo asked now.

Cosmo nodded, happy to be of service. "Up until now, we've only ever gone out to sea for a few hours at a time, and always closely watched by the teaching captains. But tomorrow, everything changes. We set sail as five independent yacht crews to complete forty-eight hours of sailing and a number of challenges, designed to test our BRONTE skills!"

"BRONTE skills?" Neo's face was awash with confusion.

Ocean took over. "B-R-O-N-T-E. Bravery, Resilience, Observation, Navigation, Teamwork and general Excellence."

Captain Kirstin Larsen, who was running just ahead of them, now turned and shook her head, flicking out her neat blonde bob. "If you can say all those words whilst running, Barracudas, you are *not* running fast enough!" There was steel in her fjord-blue eyes. "Come on, guys! I know you're all excited for Oceans Bound, but step it up!"

As the captain turned around and sped on her athletic way, the five Barracudas fell silent. Jasmine heard the sound of a metal blade striking the ground as Leif Larsen – Captain Larsen's son – powered forward to join the group. Due to an encounter with a shark, Leif wore a prosthetic below his left knee. Now, as he often did for sports and other activities, he had switched out his regular prosthetic for a blade.

"I think Mor missed her Seamoss Smoothie this morning!" he whispered to Jasmine.

Jasmine giggled. She was impressed how Leif managed to maintain the fine balance of loyalty towards both his teacher mum and his mates.

"She's safely out of hearing," Leif informed the others.

"You can continue briefing Neo!"

Cosmo tapped Neo on the arm and pointed out past the glittering harbour to the ocean beyond. "We sail off in a north-east direction towards that archipelago of small islands over there."

"And all along the way," Ocean continued, "we get set challenges by the teachers."

"The captains record everything in Logbooks," Jacoby said. "And, at the end, there are bonus marks for arriving first at target destinations, as well as

overcoming challenging sailing conditions or showing special initiative."

"Do the teachers follow us to see how we're doing?" Neo asked.

Jasmine shook her head. "The challenges are laid out in advance by some of the older students."

"We know that the teachers *do* keep tabs on our progress," Ocean added. "But we're not entirely sure how."

Jasmine imagined this was a lot for Neo to take in.

"Those are the basics," Cosmo resumed. "But what matters, Neo, is that Oceans Bound really shows each of us – and our teachers – just what we're made of. How well we've learnt our lessons. And, *crucially*, which of us has leadership potential."

They were nearing the end of their 5k loop, back to the terrace they had set off from. Captain Larsen was already at the water station, chatting away with Captains Pavel Platonov and Victor Molina, both of whom had led the 10k run with the Academy's older students.

"Everything we have said so far is just background information," Leif told Neo. "Because all any of us really care about is *who* the five captains are going to be. Isn't that right, Jacoby?"

"I don't know what you're talk—" Jacoby began.

"Argh!" Jasmine cried loudly over him. "Somebody make him stop!"

"Don't go there, Blunt," Cosmo grinned. "We all know it's been your only waking thought for weeks, if not months, now."

"Maybe," Jacoby admitted, sounding cross. "But is it really such a terrible thing that I want to be one of the five captains? The truth is, there isn't a Barracuda among us who *doesn't* want to be a captain." His eyes ranged across his fourteen classmates. "Anyone who says they don't is a liar, a rogue . . . and a scoundrel!"

Jasmine and her friends all laughed at Jacoby's over-the-top language. He sounded just like his dad, Captain Beaufort Blunt.

"Well, Jacoby," Captain Platonov said. It seemed the teaching captains had witnessed his outburst. "If you're so keen to find out who the five chosen captains are, you had better go shower and have breakfast. Commodore Kuo and Captain Salt will reveal the five names at assembly in The Octopus precisely one hour from now." He smiled. "So you will soon be put out of your misery."

"Or," Cosmo said, "you might be much *more* miserable!" He nudged Jacoby in the ribs.

"Ouch!" Jacoby complained. He prepared to launch a revenge attack but froze as Captain Larsen shot him a warning look.

"I'd think very carefully about what you do or say next," Captain Larsen told him. "Always remember, the head and deputy head have eyes and ears everywhere – and decisions can be overturned right up until the last minute."

Jacoby folded his arms, thoughtfully. "That's very interesting. Thank you, Captain Larsen." His eyes were bright.

Jasmine knew exactly what he was thinking. She really hoped they *did* make Jacoby one of the five captains. She knew him so well – maybe better than he knew himself – and she wasn't sure how he'd cope with the disappointment of not being chosen.

Actually, she *was* sure.

He'd be a total nightmare.

CHAPTER 3
DREAMS OF GLORY

Sitting between his roommate Wing and Neo in The Octopus, Jacoby felt his nerves soar to new heights. All one hundred and fifty students, from across each of the ten years, were gathered in Pirate Academy's main hall. Nothing unusual in that – the students came here every morning for assembly. But you could feel today that something was different. There was a powerful sense of expectation in the air.

Jacoby's eyes landed on the vast flag which hung at the back of the stage. It bore the Pirate Academy logo, made up of a sword, compass, anchor and pearl. Each symbol spoke to one of the key talents required to be a great pirate. The sword stood for courage and the ability to fight your corner. The compass symbolised your skill at navigation – both out at sea and through life's fiercest challenges. The anchor was a reminder to ground yourself in the history of piracy and draw

inspiration from those who came before. The pearl was perhaps the most important of all: marking your talent at tackling the toughest situations and finding the power to unlock the treasure within them.

As the teaching captains walked in and took their seats on the stage, the students rose to their feet. Jacoby scanned the faces of the captains for clues. Commodore Kuo and Captain Salt made the final decision about who would be captains for Oceans Bound. Still, Jacoby knew that each of the teachers would have said who they thought were the best candidates.

Jacoby was worried after his disastrous report at the last Captains' Evening. He had worked hard to turn things around in the weeks since then – paying better attention in Navigation lessons (even when it made his head hurt!) and taking more care with his sums in Treasure Class. He knew too that his role in rescuing Neo from the evil League of True Pirates had not gone unnoticed. But still, had he done enough to claw his way back?

His eyes now fell on the five empty chairs at the front of the stage. They were reserved for the Oceans Bound captains. His gaze zeroed in on one of the chairs and he pictured himself sitting there proudly, twenty minutes from now, in front of all his fellow students.

Jacoby saw that Miss Martingale had taken her position at the vast pipe organ to the starboard side of the stage. The Octopus was filled with the stirring introductory notes to the Pirate Federation anthem. Jacoby rose to his feet to join the others in singing the inspiring old song:

I pledge my life to adventure,
I submit my soul to the sea.
I shall fight both wind and weather,
For the dream that burns in me.
And the dream that burns in me
Is simply to be free.
And there is no greater freedom than
To be a pirate!

Jacoby felt as if he was hearing the words of the anthem for the very first time. There truly *was* no greater freedom than to be a pirate! Feeling moved, he glanced up above him to the high-domed ceiling of The Octopus. It was studded with circles of blue glass. As the morning sun sent down its rays, the room was drenched with soft blue light. It was as if they were all deep underwater. Swimming above them were what, at first glance, looked like sleek silvery fish. In fact, these were the swords of the most famous pirate captains – including those now sitting before him on the Academy stage. The legendary swords were locked securely in individual glass cases, suspended from the ceiling by almost invisible steel wires.

As Jacoby gazed up at the swords, his thoughts flashed forwards several years to the time when his own sword would hang there. Maybe someday, years from now, he would agree to give up his ocean command and return to share his wisdom with the students of the future. Ha, he'd probably be the Headcaptain! He was smiling from ear to ear as he sang:

. . . And the honour that I seek
Is a title beyond compare.
For there is no greater title than
To be a pirate!

As the anthem ended and they sat back down again, Jasmine leant forwards from the row behind. "Neo, you have such a nice singing voice," she said. Neo smiled, shyly.

"What about *me*?" Jacoby asked. "You never say anything about *my* singing!"

Jasmine fell silent for a moment, then told him. "You have an unusually loud voice, Jacoby."

Feeling peeved, Jacoby turned to watch Commodore Kuo and Captain Salt walk towards the twin lecterns at the front of the stage.

Now, Jacoby felt a fresh surge of electricity pulse through his body. You could cut the tense atmosphere in The Octopus with a rapier. Jacoby took a deep breath, crossed the fingers of both hands and, inside his socks, the toes of both feet for good measure.

He could feel his right leg jiggling wildly. His heart was racing too. He could barely breathe. Suddenly, he felt a hand on his shoulder and heard a steady voice in his ear.

"Keep calm," Jasmine whispered. "You've got this. It's your time."

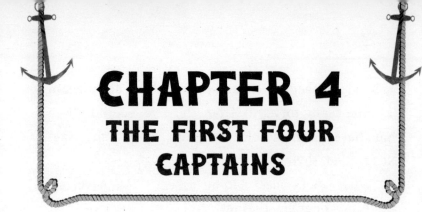

CHAPTER 4
THE FIRST FOUR CAPTAINS

"**W**ell!" Commodore Kuo's voice boomed around The Octopus. "You don't need me to remind you that this is no ordinary Academy assembly!"

The excited crowd broke into thunderous applause, cut through with delighted whoops. The Headcaptain exchanged a smile with his deputy, before continuing. "Today is a particularly thrilling one for the fifteen students in Barracuda Class." His eyes sought out their two rows. "I'm sure *you* are all keen for us to get on with things!"

"Aye, Captain!" Fergus Fairbrossen cheekily called out from along Jacoby's row. This prompted waves of laughter throughout the auditorium, including from the stage itself.

"Strictly speaking, that should be 'Aye, Commodore', Fergus!" replied the head, but his smile showed that he had enjoyed the heckle. "So," he said, adopting a more serious tone, "shall we find out the name of our first captain?"

His answer was ear-splitting applause. The head leant on his lectern, delighted, and looked across to Captain Salt who was holding up a gold envelope.

"Good luck," Neo told Jacoby, bumping his fist. They were still finessing their secret brother handshake.

The crowd hushed as Mayday Salt opened the envelope and lifted the card inside. "Our first captain for Oceans Bound is . . ."

Jacoby held his breath.

"Ocean Lermentov!"

"Yesss!" Jacoby heard a jumble of voices, including Jasmine and Cosmo's, behind him. He saw Neo turn to congratulate Ocean and realised he should probably do the same.

"Ocean, please come to the stage to receive your Captain's Logbook," the Commodore said. The sound of clapping soared again, now joined by the drumming of feet. Miss Martingale struck up the organ, with an upbeat melody, to accompany Ocean to the stage.

Jacoby watched Ocean shuffle past her fellow Barracudas to the end of the row. He found Jasmine's steady gaze on him. Knowing her well, he knew what she was trying to say to him. *Still four places to go. Stay calm.* He nodded, then turned to watch Ocean, up on stage, shake hands with the head and deputy. Next Captain Salt handed her the all-important Logbook. As Ocean held it up to the audience, there came a sudden roar from above.

Twisting around, Jacoby saw that the cry had come from Ocean's older brother, Reef Lermentov, who being in Stingray Class was a few rows behind. Reef and his pals were on their feet, performing a victory dance for Ocean. Was that entirely necessary?

"Are you ready for another?" Commodore Kuo now asked the crowd. Their rapt response left him in no doubt. He turned to Captain Salt, who reached for the next gold envelope.

"Our second captain," Captain Salt announced, "is Leif Larsen!"

Jacoby glanced to his left, in time to see Leif stand and receive a hearty double-sided hug from the Fairbrossen twins.

"Come on down!" the head invited Leif. Jacoby watched as, on stage, the other teachers congratulated Captain Larsen. Jacoby was genuinely delighted for

Leif. Some people might think Leif had an unfair advantage, because his mum was a teacher here, but those people were just bad sports!

"Two down, three to go!" The Commodore announced. "I wonder who's next?"

"Well let's see!" Captain Salt's warm eyes shimmered as she lifted the next gold envelope.

Jacoby held his breath once more. *This time*, said the voice inside his head. *You've waited long enough. It's your turn . . . Jacoby Blunt!*

There was a fresh roar of applause, the biggest so far. Was this really all for him?! Jacoby rose to his feet, feeing strangely warm and giddy. As he did so, he noticed Ari Kailis smiling happily as she danced to the end of the row.

"What are you doing?" Cosmo hissed from behind him. "Why are *you* standing up?"

Jacoby felt a chill wave of disappointment, followed by a flood of embarrassment at his awful mistake. "Go, Ari!" he called, fist-punching the air above his head. "Great result! Richly deserved!" It seemed to take an age to lower himself back down into his chair.

"Well, now, I wonder," the Commodore's eyes twinkled, "who is going to be our fourth captain?"

He glanced at Captain Salt, who shrugged.

Jacoby told himself to stay calm. *There are still two more spots to go . . . and don't they always leave the best to last?*

"Kazuo Watanabe!" Captain Salt announced.

Unlike the others, Kaz seemed totally shocked that he'd been chosen. Jacoby was struck by his classmate's modesty. When it was his turn, he'd try to give off those vibes too. For now, he gave Kaz a thumbs-up and called, "Congrats!"

"Thanks!" Kaz grinned, before slipping off to make his way down to the stage, to the backing track of more feverish cheering and fresh beats from Miss Martingale.

The general mob of students had grown louder with each of the four announcements. But, as Kaz walked across the stage, Jacoby realised that the Barracudas had all now fallen quiet. It was as if it had dawned on them all at once. There was only one chair left – just one captain left to be announced. They were, as Captain Molina liked to say, at the pointy end.

"Well," he heard the head's voice. "There's just one more gold envelope."

Jacoby felt himself start to shiver with fresh nerves. Neo sent him a reassuring smile. Then he felt a hand squeeze his left shoulder. It was Cosmo. Then Jasmine placed her hand on his right shoulder. Jacoby lifted his own hands to clasp those of his friends. They were in this together. As much as they all wanted this for themselves, they were here for each other.

He watched as Captain Salt lifted the fifth gold envelope into the light. She held it there for a moment. Jacoby's gaze moved to the flag at the back of the stage – noting the sword, the compass, the anchor, the pearl – then to the smiling faces of the teaching captains and on to his four chosen classmates sitting on the stage. His eyes returned to Captain Salt, just in time to see her remove the card and break into a delighted smile.

"Our fifth and final captain is . . ."

CHAPTER 5
CAPTAIN NUMBER FIVE

"Jasmine Peacock!"

No. No. No. This cannot be happening.

Jasmine felt the eyes of her classmates all turn towards her. They were smiling at her, so happy for her success. All except one.

She felt Jacoby's hand slip out of her own. He didn't turn around, like Neo and Wing. He folded his arms, slumping deeper into his chair.

"Congratulations, Jasmine!" Cosmo jumped to his feet and stretched out his hand. "No one deserves this more than you!" He squeezed her hand reassuringly – as if he could tell how shaky she was feeling.

"Jasmine, come down and collect your Logbook!" the head called from the stage. Numbly, Jasmine moved along the row. Shay, Layla, Rose and Carmen each lifted their hands and offered hearty congratulations. High-fiving them, she did her best to return their smiles. But she felt sick. She knew how much Jacoby had wanted this.

Then, as she made her way down to the stage, something clicked inside Jasmine's head. *I deserve this*, she told herself. *I've worked hard and I'm talented. And a friend should be happy when their friend succeeds – not go into a sulk.*

By the time she reached the stage, her numbness had given way to a fizzy excitement. She strode forwards to shake the headcaptain's hand, feeling like she was floating on air. "Well done, Jasmine!" the head said, smiling warmly at her. "You're going to make a terrific captain."

Beaming, Captain Salt gave Jasmine a hug, before handing over her blue Captain's Log. There was a roar of applause as Jasmine took it. Then, heart pounding, she walked over to join her four fellow Barracudas at the front. They were all up on their feet. Ocean and Ari were arm-in-arm, jumping up and down with excitement.

"We did it!" Ocean cried as Jasmine joined them. "I told you we would. And we did!"

Out of the corner of her eye, Jasmine noticed Captain van Amstel make a dash to the port side of the stage. What was he up to? Her question was swiftly answered as blue, white and silver streamers showered over the five excited Barracudas.

"Well done, Jasmine!" Kaz said, as a blue streamer attached to the tip of his nose. She found herself folded into a group hug. Then they stood together, facing a wall of noise.

"There they are," Commodore Kuo's voice boomed. "Your five chosen captains!"

Jasmine stared out at the rows of seats. Everyone was on their feet now. Her eyes found Neo, who grinned and brought his fingers to his lips to whistle. Jasmine saw that Jacoby was also now standing. But, as her eyes met his, he didn't smile. He refused to hold her gaze, dropping his eyes to the floor. She felt sad but also angry.

"Well," she heard Mayday Salt say at her side. "It's time we whisked you five away for your Captains' Briefing. The countdown to Oceans Bound begins right here, right now."

With that, Captain Salt strode off the stage into the wings to the starboard side. As the five chosen captains lingered on stage, a fresh shower of streamers fell over them. Jasmine stood there, gazing out at her fellow students through the paper rainstorm. It did strange things to her vision but she suddenly caught sight of a cloaked figure standing in the aisle towards the back of the auditorium. Her breath caught in her chest.

Straining her eyes to see through the falling streamers and the spotlights directed at the stage, Jasmine watched the figure walk down the aisle until it was standing in the light. The hood fell away and a man smiled at her, then lifted his hands to join in the clapping.

Jasmine's heart missed a beat. What was Uncle Noah doing here? Wasn't he supposed to be locked up in a cell, under 24/7 guard, in the Pirate Federation's maximum-security prison? Even if, by some miracle, he had found a way to escape, why on oceans would he have come here – to the Academy?

"Do you see him?" Jasmine asked Ocean.

"See who?" her friend asked, sounding confused.

Jasmine found it somehow impossible to speak her uncle's name. Instead, she just pointed to where he stood. "Him. There, in the middle of the aisle."

Ocean gripped her friend's hand tightly. "Roomie, there's nobody there."

And as Jasmine peeled away a stray silver streamer from her eyelid, she saw that Ocean was right. The aisle was empty.

CHAPTER 6
A CHOICE AND A WARNING

Jasmine sat with the other four Oceans Bound captains in a semi-circle in the main room of the Barracuda Clubhouse. Facing them was Captain Salt, who – with the aid of the whiteboard behind her and numerous hand-outs – was talking them through the detailed workings of Oceans Bound weekend. Jasmine's pen was poised over her open notebook, as though she was paying close attention. But her mind was far away.

Was it possible she had only imagined Uncle Noah? He had seemed *so* real.

Jasmine's head ached. She was aware she had been under a lot of stress for weeks now, ever since her parents' ship had failed to show up for Captains' Evening.

Jasmine's beloved parents had been officially Missing At Sea since that time. Jasmine had experienced painfully clear visions of the ship she knew so well caught in a terrible storm and her brave parents doing all they could to save the ship and their crew. Jasmine had no evidence that *The Blue Marlin* had in fact sailed into a storm – but still the vision kept coming back to her, both in her feverish dreams and, strangely worse, during the daytime.

Mayday Salt had insisted Jasmine check in with her regularly. Jasmine had drawn comfort from the chats the two had, over cups of sweet passionflower tea, in the deputy head's study. Captain Salt told her she was coping brilliantly with all the stress and uncertainty. Jasmine wasn't so sure. Her thoughts scuttled back to Uncle Noah, standing in the aisle of The Octopus, smiling at her and clapping. It made no logical sense. But wasn't that just Uncle Noah's style?

"Does anyone have any questions, so far?" She heard Mayday's voice now, though it seemed to come from a long distance away, as if Jasmine had dived deep underwater.

"Jasmine?" This time, the voice was closer. "You've been unusually quiet. Any questions?"

"No," Jasmine said, shaking her head. "No questions." She glanced across at Ocean, realising that she was going to need a full debrief from her roommate later.

"Oh-kay," Captain Salt said slowly, her gaze lingering on Jasmine.

Fortunately, just then, there was a loud knock on the door of the Barracuda Clubhouse.

"Word reached me that you've got to the exciting part," said Commodore Kuo, his eyes full of mystery.

Jasmine was finally paying attention to her surroundings. She noticed that the long banqueting table that stretched along the centre of the Clubhouse had, all this time, been covered with a deep blue cloth. But the surface was not flat but decidedly bumpy.

"Shall I do the honours?" the head asked his deputy.

Captain Salt nodded. "Yes please, Headcaptain!"

Smiling, the head reached out and, with the air of a magician, tugged at the corner of the blue cloth. It came away in his hand, revealing what lay underneath. Ten small wood-and- brass treasure chests had been laid out on the table. Jasmine and the other young captains rose to their feet.

"Interesting, huh?" Captain Salt said. Rising from her chair, she began setting down name-cards in front of each of the chests.

Lewis, Wing, Carmen, Fergus, Layla, Rose, Shay, Cosmo, Neo, Jacoby.

The names of the remaining ten Barracudas. All those who had *not* been chosen as captains.

The Commodore smiled. "Captains, it's time to invite your classmates to join your crew."

Captain Salt handed each of the young captains two thick plain cards. "Each of you will invite two members of Barracuda Class to be your crewmates. You will write a short note to them, telling them why you would value their contribution. You will then give your cards to me and I will place the invitations in the treasure chest bearing that student's name. Then, after you have all gone, we'll invite the other Barracudas back in to collect their invites." Mayday's bright eyes now met each of the OB Captains' in turn. "Think carefully about who you want on your team. This is not simply about friendship. It's about who will make the most effective crew for your expedition."

Jasmine felt her breath catch in her chest, as she twirled her pen in her fingers. She had to get this right.

***

"All done?" Mayday enquired.

Jasmine glanced up to nod and passed over her two cards. The deputy head didn't look at the names – she simply walked on to take Kaz's choices. Once she had collected everyone's cards, Mayday turned to face them. "Excellent work, Captains! It's been quite a morning for you five. You now have free time until afternoon lessons."

***

"How intense was that?" Kaz exclaimed, as the five Oceans Bound captains stepped back out into the sunlight.

Leif nodded. "On a scale of one to ten, I'd give it a twenty!"

Ari smiled. "Well, as a reward, how about we take advantage of our free time and have a swim?"

Everyone agreed this was a great idea. They set off back in the direction of Barracuda Block, where their cabins were, to get changed into their swimming things.

Ari, Kaz and Ocean chatted away excitedly. Jasmine hung back.

"Is everything OK?" Leif asked her, gently. "I hope you don't feel guilty because you're captain and . . . *he's* not? You really deserve this."

Jasmine smiled. "Thanks," she said. "And no, it's not about . . . Jacoby. I *am* excited. This morning has just been a lot – even by our standards!"

Leif smiled kindly at her, his blue eyes sparkling. "If you ever need to talk, I'm here for you."

Jasmine nodded, feeling grateful to have such supportive friends.

Reaching Barracuda Block, they headed off to their cabins. As Ari disappeared with a wave into Cabin 7, Jasmine and Ocean continued on to Cabin 9. Jasmine pushed open the door . . .

. . . and immediately slipped on an envelope, lying on the floor near the entrance.

"Careful, roomie!" Ocean said. "We don't want any accidents *before* Oceans Bound even begins."

As Ocean closed the door, Jasmine stared at the envelope. Her name was written on it, but she did not recognise the handwriting. The envelope had not been sealed, simply tucked in. Inside was a card – not too different from the one they had written their crew invites on earlier. But this note was not a thoughtful invitation. Quite the opposite, in fact.

Jasmine read the words, feeling shockwaves pass through her. Then, as if the card was red hot, she let it fall to the floor. Frowning, Ocean leapt across and swept it up in her hands. Together they stared at the jagged writing:

WARNING: DON'T GO ON OCEANS BOUND WEEKEND, JASMINE. OR IT WILL END VERY BADLY FOR YOU AND ALL CONCERNED. YOUR FREINDS AT LOT P

CHAPTER 7
THE TREASURE CHESTS

"Look, I get it," Neo told Jacoby, as they tramped across the sun-drenched Academy gardens towards the Barracuda Clubhouse. "You really, *really* wanted to be Captain."

"Not just *wanted*, Neo. *Deserved*. I've been working so hard, so long, for this."

As if to rub salt into Jacoby's wounds, they now saw the five OB Captains striding off towards the Academy lagoon, carrying their swimming towels, laughing and joking.

"Sorry to be blunt," Neo continued, "no pun intended – but I think you just have to accept this blow and move on."

Jacoby looked hurt.

"Maybe I was a bit *too* blunt," Neo said.

"You're my *broth—*", Jacoby began, but, seeing Cosmo approach, swallowed the rest of the forbidden word.

"You're supposed to be on *my* side!"

Neo frowned. Mostly, he loved the fact that he and Jacoby were brothers. But now Jacoby *always* expected Neo to take his side. This was making Neo uncomfortable. After all, he had known Jasmine, Leif, Ocean, Shay and all the other Barracudas just as long as he had known Jacoby, despite their special – and, for now, secret – connection.

"Here we go!" Cosmo boomed, as they walked under the grapevine-covered entrance to the Clubhouse. "Time to find out who's top of the invite list and who's Not Wanted on Voyage!"

***

The ten Barracudas were gathered along the length of the table. The ten wood-and-brass treasure chests, with their name cards in front of them, were laid out before them.

"Let's begin, shall we?" Captain Salt's commanding voice drew Neo's attention. "Earlier, the five Oceans Bound captains each wrote invites to two of you to join their three-person crew." She pointed. "I have placed those invitations in the treasure chests in front of you."

"What about those of us who don't have any invites?"

Cosmo enquired, a wicked grin blooming on his face. "Asking for a friend!"

"Excellent question, Cosmo!" Captain Salt nodded. "For now, I have inserted blank cards into those chests with no actual invites. I trust this will maintain secrecy and prevent any unwanted embarrassment. Please remember this is only the start of crew recruitment. Once the first crew members are agreed, we will move on to phase two. "

Cosmo leant closer to hiss in Neo's ear. "Also known as the mop-up exercise!"

"We've been running Oceans Bound for thirteen years now," Mayday added, her eyes lingering on Cosmo. "And, in that time, nobody has ever been left off a crew. So, whether you have several invitations or none at all, please just trust the process!"

Neo found himself hesitating. He knew he had good reason to. Taking a breath, he lifted the lid and saw a blank card.

He wasn't surprised and not at all disappointed. After all, he was still the new kid. He lifted the blank card out of his treasure chest. As he did so, he realised that this card was only the top of quite a thick pile. Handwriting covered the card underneath. Smiling, he turned one card on top of the next. Under the decoy blank card, there were *three* invitations to join a captain's crew. *Not half bad for the new kid!*

Of the three invitations, Neo knew right away which one he *would* have chosen to accept. *If* he had been able to join his classmates on Oceans Bound weekend. He'd been putting off saying anything right up until this point, but he couldn't delay much longer.

CHAPTER 8
CREW
MANOEUVRES

The first crew to declare was Ari's. It happened at lunch. A loud whoop came from the edge of the terrace where Ari, Layla and Rose were jumping up and down in excitement. "First crew declared!" they shouted in unison.

Jasmine stood up, along with the other Barracudas, to clap and cheer them. Across from her, Jacoby muttered to Cosmo. "No surprises on Crew Ari then!"

***

The second crew to announce was Ocean's. This time it was Cosmo himself who interrupted Navigation Class to cry, "Second crew declared!"

"Just so we're clear," Captain Larsen said, a twinkle in her eye. "This is *Ocean's* crew, yes?"

Her comment was met with laughter from the rest of the class. Ocean stepped forwards. "Yes, it's *my* crew and I've recruited the super-talented Shay and Cosmo."

Beaming, she looped her arms around the shoulders of her two crewmates.

"Excellent news!" Captain Larsen said, with a nod. "Now, do we have any other crews ready to declare?" Her bright eyes swept across the room but no one spoke. Jasmine caught Jacoby smiling strangely at her but, when she met his gaze, he looked away. Captain Larsen clapped her hands. "In that case, Barracudas, back to your navigation charts!"

***

At the start of Marine Biology, the Barracudas' final lesson of the day, Leif called across the water, "Third crew declared!" Like the rest of his classmates, he was currently waist deep in ocean water, collecting seaweed specimens. On either side of him stood Wing and Lewis.

"My crew!" Leif announced proudly, before dropping slimy tendrils of seaweed over each of their shoulders.

"Yuck! Is it too late to switch?" Wing cried out, brushing the seaweed away.

"I'm afraid so," confirmed Captain van Amstel. "Just two crews left to declare! At this rate, we might have all the OB crews sorted by the end of the day." Nodding and smiling, he straightened his spectacles and waded over to inspect Leif's crew's seaweed haul.

Ocean was working close by Jasmine. "Any updates on *your* crew?" Ocean asked.

"Nothing so far," Jasmine told her.

Ocean squeezed her arm. "That might be about to change!" Jasmine looked up to find Neo wading purposefully towards her. "Time to make myself scarce," Ocean said. "But you know how good my hearing is!"

"Thought you could maybe use some help?" Neo said, as he reached Jasmine's side. "Actually, that's a total fib. I thought this might be a good chance for us to talk."

"Sure," she said, casually reaching out for a long strand of seaweed.

Neo's kind eyes locked onto hers. "Well, firstly, I wanted to say thank you *so much* for inviting me to join your crew." He broke off, looking suddenly awkward.

"It's OK," Jasmine told him. "You've obviously had other invitations."

Neo lowered his voice. "You *are* my top choice, Jasmine. I'd have loved to join your crew."

She narrowed her eyes, unsure exactly what he was telling her.

"I'm pulling out of Oceans Bound weekend. In fact, I'm thinking of pulling out of the Academy altogether." He looked upset and relieved at the same time.

"I don't understand," she said. "Why?"

Neo sighed. "I've been having these terrible nightmares," he told her. "I thought if I gave it time they would go away, but actually they're getting worse. They're always about the night Mum died, when the League of True Pirates boarded our ship. I discover her . . . body, and then I race to hide somewhere in her cabin. It's totally terrifying, just like that awful night."

Jasmine felt the terrible weight of his words. She understood some of what he was going through. "I'm so, so sorry, Neo."

"And then, perhaps you've noticed how weird I get during sailing class?"

"Weird? No. How?"

"Kind of jumpy, I guess. And when we're out on the water, I feel *so* seasick. I was never seasick one day in my life until . . . well, you know." He frowned. "So you see, I just can't go on Oceans Bound. I'd be no use on your crew. And I need to think hard about the best place for me to be."

"Neo!" Jasmine said, gently but firmly enough to regain his attention. "I have nightmares too. And the horrible visions don't only come at night, but sometimes during the day." It was a help to share this with him.

"It's not the same. You found your mother . . . dead. My parents are only missing. But they have been missing for over a month now and, although I try to keep my hope alive, it's really hard."

Neo nodded, his face full of kindness. "Jasmine, I am so, so sorry about your parents. Of course, you must be going wild with worry." He paused. "You truly are amazing. I don't know how you manage to hold everything together."

Jasmine shook her head. "I'm *barely* holding it together. I'm doing my best in classes and with my homework. But, honestly, there are days when I feel like giving up and just staying in bed."

Neo shook his head. "I'd never have guessed. You're going to make a great captain!"

"The thing is, I can't be much of a captain without a crew. So, how about it?" She smiled. "I'm asking you to be brave . . . but only as brave as I'm asking myself to be. If there's a way you *can* come on Oceans Bound, I know we will find a way to support each other if things get tough. She quickly corrected herself. "*When* things get tough."

Jasmine paused to give him a moment. He did seem to be weighing it up.

"As for your seasickness, that's an easy one," she continued. "We need to go see Nurse Carmichael. She'll be able to give you a pill or an injection or something."

Neo shuddered. "No needles, thank you! I'd much rather have a pill."

Jasmine nodded. "So that's what we'll tell Nurse C. I'll go with you later if you like."

Neo shook his head. "You'd do that for me?"

"If that's what it takes to get you on my crew," she said, carefully.

His eyes met hers. "Jasmine, I've been on your crew for approximately the past five minutes."

***

By the time it came to get ready for bed, neither of the two remaining crews had been declared. Changing into her favourite pyjamas, Jasmine thought how frustrated she was with Jacoby. It seemed to her that he had been giving her the runaround all afternoon.

Ocean stepped out of the bathroom, smelling minty fresh. Seeing Jasmine's face, she sighed. "I know you're fed up. Why's Blunt holding out on you?"

"That's easy," Jasmine said. "Pride."

Ocean smiled and nodded. Just then, there was a

knock on their cabin door. The roommates' eyes met. Ocean signalled she would greet their visitor.

"Jacoby Blunt!" Ocean exclaimed loudly. "What a totally unexpected surprise!"

He smiled tightly at Ocean then glanced past her. "Jasmine, are you free for a word?"

"You've left it quite late!" Ocean said, stepping aside so that Jacoby could enter their cabin. "Oh gosh," she exclaimed. "I've suddenly remembered I need to brush my teeth . . . again!"

Once they were alone, Jacoby looked awkwardly at Jasmine, but said nothing.

"Is there something you want to tell me?" she asked him.

He shrugged, glancing about the room. "I suppose I just wanted to say thank you for inviting me to join your crew." He stroked his chin. "I really appreciate the offer. And, well, I'm going to think over my remaining invitations tonight and make a final decision."

Remaining invitations? How many had he received? *Final decision?* Was he suggesting he'd already turned one captain down? This was beyond cheeky, even by Blunt standards. And, frankly, the maths didn't stack up.

"Well, OK then," Jasmine said, folding her arms tightly. "Thanks for letting me know."

Ocean flung open the bathroom door. "So, what did I miss?"

Before Jacoby could speak, Jasmine told her, "Jacoby is having a really careful think about which crew he'd prefer to join."

Ocean grinned. "Well don't think about it *too* long, Jacoby. We set sail tomorrow!"

"Yes, I'm very much aware of that fact, thank you," Jacoby said, turning to leave.

But, as he turned, something caught his eye. The terrible note from LOT P. Lying on Jasmine's desk.

"What's this?" he asked, grabbing it in his hands.

"I think you can probably work out what it is," Ocean said, lifting it back out of his grasp. "A nasty little threat which we are choosing to completely ignore."

"Ignore?" Jacoby said. "Is that wise?" His eyes were wide as portholes. "Shouldn't the Commodore or Captain Salt see this? Shouldn't you think twice about setting sail for OB?"

Jasmine shook her head. "Nothing and no one is keeping me from Oceans Bound."

"Exactly!" Ocean declared, spinning Jacoby around

and leading him to the doorway. "Night, night Jacoby. I do hope you get some sleep in between pondering your decision." She closed the cabin door tightly.

Jasmine sighed. "I feel bad for him, Ocean. He wanted so badly to be a captain. What should I do?"

Ocean grinned again. "I'm not as patient or as kind a person as you, roomie. What *I'd* do is get some sleep and leave Jacoby to toss and turn. And then, in the morning, I'd get up nice and early and invite Fergus Fairbrossen to complete my crew."

CHAPTER 9
TERRIBLE NEWS

"I came as soon as I could, Headcaptain," Captain Salt told Commodore Kuo as she stepped into the head's office. "Whatever's happened?" she asked.

The head gripped the earpiece of his blue phone tightly in his right hand. Mayday knew that the Commodore only received calls about high-level crises on the blue phone. She closed the office door carefully behind her and strode over to where he was sitting, frozen, on the edge of his desk.

The headcaptain replaced the earpiece of the blue phone in its cradle and rose to his feet. "Noah Ripley has escaped."

"Escaped? But that's impossible. There *is* no escape from Warspite Cove."

"So we thought," the head nodded, solemnly. "So we

believed. And yet it seems that Ripley, and his wretched accomplices, found a way." His eyes met hers. "And now, they are back at large, out on the oceans, doubtless preparing their next exercise in evil."

Mayday slumped down on the head's leather sofa. "Of course, we'll have to cancel Oceans Bound," she said. "What a terrible sha—"

"Now let's not be overly hasty!" the head said, swinging his body around to face her. "Let's not start cancelling anything just yet."

Mayday's eyes blazed across at him. "But, John, we have to! To send our Barracudas out to sea for forty-eight hours, unaccompanied, with these dangerous rebels at large . . . Well, it's just inviting danger, surely?"

The head made a tight fist, a strange light in his eyes – like a lighthouse flashing from a distant shore. "You'll forgive me if I see things just a tad differently."

Mayday's eyes narrowed. Sometimes the headcaptain worked in mysterious ways indeed. She took a breath, cleared her throat, then asked: "How *do* you see this?"

Commodore Kuo rose to his feet and began pacing up and down in front of his treasured old painting of his much younger self. "Oceans Bound has always been an important rite of passage for our Year 5 students.

After their first few years of training, it's where we get to see what they are truly made of, out there on their own."

"Precisely," Mayday cut in. "Out there *on their own*. But if the Barracudas set sail tomorrow, they won't be at sea alone. They'll be out there with this dangerous new enemy – about whom we know so very little – waiting in the shadows and the shallows."

"That's highly poetic!" the Commodore said, approvingly. "But I strongly suspect that Ripley and his comrades have bigger fish to fry than our young Barracudas."

"Fair point," Mayday conceded. "Though, remember, Ripley's last act was the kidnap of Neo Splice . . . and Priyanka Swift." Her dark eyes met the headcaptain's.

"We always closely monitor the Barracudas' progress during Oceans Bound." The head was defiant. "We can add in some extra security measures this time around."

"What kind of measures?" Mayday enquired.

"Plenty of time to work out the details later," the head said, with a wave of his hand. In Mayday's experience, this meant that details might *or might not* be worked out later.

"I won't lie to you, John," she told him. "I'm worried."

"I know." He nodded, smiling. "I'm an optimist. You're a pessimist. It's why we make such a great team!"

"I'm a *realist*," Mayday said, firmly. "And I am really worried about Jasmine Peacock. Ripley is her uncle. What if he tries to make contact with her or, worse, attempts to kidnap her?"

"Well, we certainly won't allow that to happen!" The Commodore was adamant. "But you make an excellent point. Ripley might well seek out his niece. And, when he does . . . bingo! We'll have him back in Federation custody and, this time, no cosy cell at Warspite Cove."

Mayday frowned. There *were* no cosy cells at Warspite Cove. It was the Pirate Federation's highest security prison. If Noah Ripley had found a way to escape from there, he could be depended upon to escape from *anywhere* – be it a locked metal chest, bound in iron chains, deposited at the very bottom of the ocean.

"Jasmine has been through so much," Mayday persisted. "Her parents have been missing for over a month now. We have no concrete intelligence as to their fate or whereabouts. She's hanging by a thread, John . . . At the very least, we have to tell her what's happened."

"You think?" His eyes narrowed.

Mayday nodded, firmly. "No question. First thing in the morning, I'll meet with her, bring her up to speed and offer her the chance to opt out of Oceans Bound."

The head frowned. "Well, all right," he agreed. "That's a sound plan. But I'll be joining that meeting."

CHAPTER 10
REALLY IMPORTANT, REALLY URGENT

Jasmine sat on the bench at the top of Swashbuckle Hill. It was one of her favourite places to come and think. She liked it best in the early morning, before anyone else was about.

She had had another restless night, tossing and turning with thoughts and worries. Firstly, there was the question of what to do about Jacoby. Ocean's advice had been clear – to *uninvite* Jacoby from her crew and recruit Fergus instead. Jasmine wasn't sure she could be so harsh with Jacoby. All the same, he had upset her – and also made her cross.

Jasmine was worried too about Neo. It made her desperately sad to think that he had been close to pulling out of Oceans Bound and that he was thinking about leaving Pirate Academy. It made complete sense that the brutal death of his mother was preying on his mind but to leave the Academy so soon . . .

Didn't he feel safe here? Did he feel his being here was making it less safe for the others? There was still so much she didn't know about Neo. She hoped their chat had been a bit of help. And Nurse Carmichael had said that she would see him this morning to find a solution to his seasickness.

Threaded through everything was Jasmine's worry about her parents. She had brought her mum's silver music box with her, up to the top of the hill. She lifted it now and turned it upside down, so she could see her mum's scratched, coded message.

Your father and I are safe!
Hold tight and we will talk soon.

"I'm trying, mum," Jasmine said out loud. "I'm doing my best! But *where* are you?"

She saw a droplet of water fall onto the metal surface of the music box, blurring her mum's message. Her first thought was that it must be starting to rain. It took another two or three droplets to fall before she realised she was crying.

She set the box down again and reached into her pocket for a hankie. Drying her eyes, she looked up to find she was no longer alone. Someone was standing right in front of her.

"We need to talk," he said.

***

"You need to talk," Nurse Carmichael told Neo, sitting across from him in her cosy office. "Talking's the best cure in the world at times like this." Her voice had a reassuring lilt to it. Neo liked it – almost as much as he liked the homemade biscuits she had given him, alongside a comfortingly sweet cup of tea.

"I mean it, Neo," she said. "You made a powerful breakthrough when you told Jasmine how you were feeling. I want you to do more of that. A *lot* more. I know you are only just getting to know your classmates. But you have good instincts – so pick the right people and don't be afraid to tell them what's on your mind. This is how friendships develop."

Neo nodded thoughtfully, taking another nibble of the delicious shortbread finger.

"You can talk to me too," she said. "If you like."

He smiled and nodded again. "Yes, please. I *would* like that."

"Excellent. So that's our long-term plan. And now, in terms of your urgent need for something to help with seasickness . . ." She smiled and lifted the largest, longest injecting needle Neo had ever seen in his life. He did not want that going anywhere near his body! Maybe it was better to just risk throwing up?

"Know what they call this?" Nurse Carmichael asked, her eyes bright.

Neo shook his head tightly, too tense to breathe. He could only imagine the needle's horrible name.

Nurse Carmichael grinned. "My little joke, *that's* what they call this." Chuckling, she placed the needle down and rose from her chair. "Sorry, couldn't resist! I'll fetch you some anti-sickness pills. I reckon they will do the job just fine."

Neo let out a deep sigh of relief.

"Your face!" Nurse Carmichael giggled, scooping up the last piece of shortbread.

***

He had startled her, arriving out of nowhere like this.

"I'm sorry," Jacoby said, barely taking a breath.

"Sorry for so many things. For letting my need to be a captain get in the way of everything. For not properly congratulating you on becoming one . . . because you do *really* deserve this." As he spoke, he moved from one foot to the other as he often did when he was upset. "Sorry for lying to you that I was deciding between crews . . ." His face fell. "When really you were the only one to invite me."

Jasmine had suspected as much. Suspected too that he had read this as a sign of his falling popularity, when the truth was he had made himself such a pest about Oceans Bound, it was no wonder their classmates had decided to pursue safer options.

Jacoby's eyes were glistening. "You were the *only one* to invite me," he repeated. "And now I don't even feel I deserve to be on your crew. I'm *not* the best navigator. I don't think I'd be much fun to be around. And, in any case, you've probably already invited Fergus to take my place."

Jasmine froze at the mention of Fergus's name. "Jacoby, I—"

He held up his hand. "Please," he said. "I've got a bit more apologising to do."

She decided to let him continue.

"Most of all, I'm sorry that I haven't been a good enough friend to you, since your parents disappeared. It's unforgivable, Jasmine. *Unforgivable!* You've always been there for me."

"*You've* always been there for *me*," she cut in to remind him.

He shook his head. "Not these past few weeks. I want to explain . . . There are things that have happened. Big things. And I'm not ready to talk about them . . . yet. But I will be. Soon."

This was, Jasmine realised, a new phase in their friendship. Up until now, they had always shared everything with each other.

"Is everything all right?" she asked him.

He nodded. "Yes, mostly . . . but what isn't all right is the terrible way I've behaved to you. You're my best friend, Jasmine. And I am *so* sorry. I will try to do better."

"It's all right." She smiled softly. "You have been a nightmare for the past twenty-four hours. But, as we've been friends for five years, that's only a really *teensy* amount of time."

He finally stood still, his face flushed with relief. "I don't deserve a friend like you," he said.

They exchanged a smile. Then his face clouded again.

"There's just one more thing we need to talk about. The note from the League—"

Jasmine shook her head, sharply. "We don't need to talk about the note."

"But Jasmine," he began again. "You don't understand—"

"Actually, I do," she said. It hadn't taken her and Ocean long to figure out that the note had *not* come from an agent of LOT P but was, instead, the handiwork of Jacoby, with a bit of help from Cosmo – even before Ocean had forced a startled Cosmo to confess. The poor spelling of 'freinds' had been a bit of a giveaway. Jasmine thought she knew why Jacoby had done it. If his Oceans Bound was going to be ruined, then everyone else's should be too. It was a painfully clear sign of how upset he had been. He seemed calmer now and there was no need to rub any more salt into his wounds. "I do understand," she told him.

The sun was climbing fast. They needed to go get ready for the morning run and everything else the day had in store for the Barracudas. Jasmine rose to her feet, about to tell him as much, but the sight of Fergus running up the hill towards them silenced her.

"Fergus!" Jacoby exclaimed nervously, as their

classmate reached them. Jasmine could imagine the feverish thoughts now racing through Jacoby's head. But she hadn't invited Fergus to her crew and had no idea why he was here.

"Thank goodness, I've found you!" Fergus said, catching his breath. "Jasmine, you've to go to the Headcaptain's Office and meet with the Commodore and Captain Salt. ASAP."

Immediately, she felt shivers run through her. "Do you know what this is about, Fergus?"

Fergus shook his head, squinting in the sunlight as he popped his glasses onto his nose. "All I know is that it's really important, really urgent."

"I'm coming with you," Jacoby told her.

"No, it's OK, I—" She broke off, thoughts swooping around her head like wild gulls.

"I'm coming with you, Jasmine," he repeated, firmly. "Because *that's* what best friends do." Jacoby smiled. "And just to be clear, it would be my total honour to join your crew."

CHAPTER 11
THE VOTE

The door to the Headcaptain's office was ajar. Jacoby could see Captain Salt perched on the edge of the head's desk. Her face looked tight with worry but, seeing the two Barracudas, she managed a smile.

"Jasmine! Good to see you!"

Jacoby hesitated on the threshold, wondering if he would have to wait outside. But Captain Salt beckoned to him. "Jacoby, you come in too. Jasmine could do with a friend at her side."

He was pleased at the invitation, but Captain Salt's words and tone of voice left him in no doubt that something was seriously wrong. He hoped with all his heart that it wasn't horrible news about Jasmine's parents.

"I'm afraid we have some upsetting news to share," Captain Salt began, softly.

"Your uncle," Commodore Kuo cut in more noisily, then paused – as if he had a nasty taste in his mouth.

"*Noah Ripley* has escaped Pirate Federation custody."

Jacoby let out a gasp, then turned towards Jasmine. She had frozen utterly rigid.

The head looked angry. "We don't know how he did it. The prison he broke free from, along with his comrades from the League, has the highest levels of security."

"We will totally understand, Jasmine," Captain Salt said, "if, under these changed circumstances, you'd prefer to pull out of Oceans Bound weekend."

Pull out of Oceans Bound? No. Please, no . . .

"Your safety and the safety of your crew and classmates is the most important thing to us," Captain Salt continued. "There's every possibility that, having escaped, your uncle might take this opportunity to make fresh contact with you."

Jacoby now felt chills running up and down his spine. The thought of Noah Ripley seeking them out was scary – yet strangely exciting. It would give the Barracudas another chance to show just what they were made of! They had seen off LOT P agents twice before.

"We're mindful that he tried to recruit you just before he was taken away," Captain Salt told Jasmine. "We think there's every chance he might have another go."

Jasmine nodded carefully but still, frustratingly, remained silent. What *was* she thinking?

"We did consider cancelling the entire Oceans Bound expedition," Captain Salt told them.

"Yes," Commodore Kuo cut in quickly. "But we decided *not* to do that. Because it's such a massive moment in our students' journey here at the Academy. It would be a devastating disappointment all round to cancel." Catching Mayday's stare, he added, "However, we are going to heighten security levels to protect the safety of you and your classmates."

Jacoby nodded. He agreed with the Headcaptain. It would be a *disaster* if Oceans Bound did not take place! It would be like giving in to fear. And no Barracuda *ever* gave in to fear.

"But Jasmine," Mayday resumed, "there is absolutely no shame in you deciding you don't feel up to sailing, under these circumstances."

Jasmine turned towards Jacoby. It looked like she was about to ask his thoughts.

"It has to be your decision, Jasmine. We can place the crewmates you have chosen on other boats if necessary. It wouldn't be the first time we've had to send out the odd four-person crew."

At last, Jasmine spoke. Her voice was surprisingly calm. "Do I have time to think about this?"

"Not much time, I'm afraid." Captain Salt frowned. "As you know, the expedition sets sail at eleven-thirty sharp. Ahead of that, there's a lot of final prep to do."

"I understand," Jasmine said. "I really *do* want to go ahead . . ." Jacoby felt his spirits lift at her words. *Let's do this! We are Barracudas!* "But I need to talk to Neo," Jasmine continued. "His mum was killed by the League. And then he was taken hostage by Uncle Noah and his accomplices. I need to know how he feels about putting himself back in the danger zone."

"I think that's an excellent idea." Captain Salt nodded. Then she smiled. "Jasmine, whether you choose to embark on Oceans Bound or not, you are already proving a worthy captain."

The Head nodded. "Yes," he agreed. "Yes, that's right. OK, Jasmine, you go and conflab with Neo – and, *of course*, Jacoby too." He gave Jacoby a meaningful look. Jacoby frowned in confusion. Did the Head want him to try to persuade Jasmine? "And let us know your decision by . . ." He glanced at the ship-shaped clock behind his desk. "Nine o'clock?"

***

Sitting on the harbour wall, Neo listened carefully as they filled him in on the details of their meeting in the head's office. Jacoby wondered which way Neo would respond. If only they had had the opportunity for a private chat – *brother to brother* – before this.

"The three of us need to decide," Jasmine said. "We're a crew. That's how it has to be."

Neo nodded. Jacoby smiled. It was good to hear that they would all be involved. He found both his crewmates looking in his direction. It seemed they wanted him to kick things off.

"Look, I won't lie," he said. "I really want to go. But *only* if it's with the two of you – I don't want to be tacked on to anyone else's crew." To his surprise, he found himself adding, "But I know it's a more difficult decision for each of you."

Jasmine shrugged. "Not really. Imagine that LOT P is a shark. The only difference I see is that Neo and I have already both been bitten by that shark. But, make no mistake, Jacoby – if we sail out today, you'll be putting yourself in the very same line of danger."

Shivers ran through Jacoby's insides as he considered Jasmine's words. Noah Ripley and his comrades *were* as dangerous as sharks, maybe even more dangerous.

He realised that he was frightened. But a Barracuda *never* gave in to fear. "My vote is we sail."

Jasmine turned to Neo. "What about you?" Jacoby held his breath for Neo's answer.

"The way I see it," Neo said, "we didn't enrol at the Academy to shy away from danger or try to outrun fear. We came here to test ourselves in the most challenging ways and pull together to keep each other safe." His eyes were bright. "I vote we sail."

Jacoby beamed, feeling an enormous sense of brotherly pride. He couldn't have wished for a better answer from Neo. Both boys turned to Jasmine, awaiting her all-important decision.

"I agree with everything you've both said. If I let the fear of Uncle Noah stop me from sailing out today, what kind of pirate captain does that make me?" She jumped down onto the harbour. "Whatever gets thrown at us out there, I know we can handle it. I believe in this crew."

Jacoby felt joy spreading through his chest and the good type of nerves fizzing through his whole body. "So we're all agreed . . . we're sailing?" He stretched out his right hand, purposefully. The others did just the same, placing their palms one on top of the other.

"We're sailing!" Jasmine said, a smile spreading across her determined face.

"We're sailing!" the three of them repeated, palms pressing tight to each other.

CHAPTER 12
SETTING SAIL

As the Academy clock struck 11:30, Neo stood on the sun-drenched jetty, right beside Jasmine and Jacoby. They were positioned in front of the racing yacht that would be their home for the next forty-eight hours. He felt a shiver pass through him and took a breath deep from his belly, then jiggled his legs to help the feeling move on. He was nervous but also really excited.

He glanced along the dock, where the students of Barracuda Class all stood, clustered in their crews. Everyone was dressed in sailing uniforms – shorts and 'rashies' in the Barracuda's trademark aqua colour, with bright orange life vests. Neo felt his chest swell with pride under his own life vest. Any plans to leave the Academy felt a world away now. Neo thought of his mother and imagined how proud she would be, seeing him standing here in his Academy uniform alongside his new friends.

In front of the five crews of Barracudas, a rich blue carpet had been laid along the jetty.

Commodore Kuo and Captain Salt stood on a podium. At the front of the podium was a table with five coloured glass bottles – red, yellow, green, blue and purple – one for each crew. Inside each bottle was a rolled-up note, tied with ribbon. This note, once unfurled, would give each crew key instructions for their first task.

Neo glanced at the glass bottles, shimmering like jewels in the sunlight – wondering which colour bottle held the instructions for *their* crew. His gaze lifted to the ranks of Academy students, standing in their year groups, on the grass verge above the harbour wall. It was the custom for all the other students to turn out to give the Barracudas a hearty send-off on their voyage. There was a buzz of excited chatter amongst the students and also from the teaching captains, lined up along the jetty. Neo's eyes briefly met Captain Lisabeth Quivers, who gave him a reassuring wink. He smiled back, gratefully.

Everyone now fell silent as six cannons were fired from the heights of Swashbuckle Hill. Neo felt a fresh shiver run through him. This time, it was pure excitement.

"Barracudas!" The head's deep voice boomed out across the dock. "The moment has come to begin your Oceans Bound adventures!" He paused, to allow for the loud cheers and clapping from the enthusiastic crowd. "Captains, please come and collect your coloured bottles."

Neo watched as Jasmine walked over to join Ari, Kaz, Ocean and Leif in a line at the podium.

Captain Salt handed Jasmine the first coloured bottle – the blue one. "Safe travels to you and your crew," the deputy head said. Jasmine gave a neat salute before taking the bottle in her hand and stepping back into line. Jasmine's eyes met Neo's. He gave her a thumbs-up.

When all five young captains stood before the head and deputy head, each holding the all-important bottles in their eager hands, Captain Salt smiled, then spoke again.

"Our dear Barracudas,
May the waves be kind to you,
And, even when they are not so kind, be not afraid.
May the weather help speed your journey,
But, even in rough weather, keep moving forwards.
May your crew be a support to you,
Anchoring you through any challenges you meet.
May the lessons you have learnt here serve you well . . .
And now, let your Oceans Bound expedition begin!"

At this, there was a huge roar of cheers and applause, then everyone raced into action. The five captains hurried back to their crews and leapt on board their boats, hoisting the mainsails, clipping the spinnakers into position and making their final safety checks before preparing to slip their pens. Neo was aware of cheering and coloured streamers being thrown on the dock but his focus became narrow as he and Jacoby worked to loosen the knots connecting their yacht to its moorings. As Neo let the last line free and jumped over onto the boat, Jasmine smiled at her crew.

"OK," she said. "Shall we do this?"

Neo and Jacoby nodded. "Yes, Captain!"

"That's not totally necessary," Jasmine said, with a shrug. "But I'll take it."

They all moved effortlessly into their positions, with Jasmine steering the yacht out in reverse, then turning so that the sail picked up a nice flow of wind. Neo enjoyed the sense of movement as their yacht began gliding away from the jetty to the sound of cheers.

Up ahead, Ari and her crew had been the first to exit their pen. Leif and his crew were close behind, with Ocean and Kaz following in parallel. Right now, Jasmine's boat was bringing up the rear, but they had – at random – been assigned the furthest pen. Neo was confident they would make up time and speed as they moved through the harbour and beyond.

By the time they reached the far side of the harbour, poised to cross over into open ocean waters, the Barracudas' five boats were fanned out in close formation.

"Safe travels everyone!" Ocean called across from the helm of her boat.

"Go Barracudas!" cried Leif, lifting his arm high in the air.

"Go Barracudas!" came the cries of fourteen voices from across the five boats.

Neo turned to Jacoby, his eyes bright. "It's really beginning, now, isn't it?"

Jacoby nodded. He was beaming.

Jasmine passed across to Jacoby the note she had taken from the blue glass bottle. "Jacoby," she said. "You are on navigation duties, today. Think you can get us to this location?"

Jacoby scanned the note, then looked up, green-blue eyes shining. "Oh yes, Captain!"

CHAPTER 13
DIVING IN

"**R**ight here!" Jacoby declared, glancing up from his chart. "This is the spot. I'm sure of it!"

"All right then," Jasmine said, beginning the move known as a 'heave to', which would quickly bring their yacht to a stop.

Within moments, the boat had dropped all speed and was simply floating in the ocean, a short distance from a cluster of tall rocks to their port side. Now that the boat was still, Jasmine took a moment to properly take in their surroundings. It really was a beautiful spot – so tranquil. But they were not here to relax.

"Neo, are you still happy to take the dive?" she asked.

"Yes, Captain!" Neo grinned.

"OK then," she said. "Let's get you set up with some diving equipment."

Neo smiled. "How about I try a free dive?"

Jacoby's eyebrows shot up. "Someone's feeling confident!"

Neo shrugged. "I'm a fairly experienced diver. And I'll soon know if it's too deep."

"All right," Jasmine said. "I trust you."

Neo nodded, pulling off his cap, shoes and socks. "What exactly am I looking for?" he asked.

Jacoby scanned the note once more. "All it says is to 'dive down to the ocean floor and collect the instructions for the next part of your journey'."

"OK then," Neo said, with a grin. Slipping off his life vest, he pulled out a pair of goggles and slipped them over his forehead. "Wish me luck!" he said, rolling backwards off the side of the boat. There was a soft splash. Then he disappeared beneath the water's surface.

"And then there were two," Jacoby said, moving across the still boat to sit beside Jasmine.

Jasmine twisted around to look down into the ink blue waters. Just how deep a dive would Neo have to make?

"Might have guessed he'd be an amazing free diver," Jacoby said, quietly. "It seems like everyone else has hidden talents."

Jasmine turned to face him. "Jacoby, *you* have plenty of talents. You do know that, right?"

He shrugged, looking suddenly sad. "I used to think I was on the fast track to being a pirate superstar. Lately, I've had the feeling I'm just making up the numbers in Barracuda Class."

Jasmine shook her head, hating to see him so down. "You're not being fair on yourself. You're just going through a rough patch."

He looked uncertainly at her. "You really think so?"

"I *know* so," she told him. "And this weekend is the perfect opportunity to bounce back."

Turning her attention back to the water, Jasmine asked, "Should we be at all worried that Neo hasn't surfaced yet?"

Jacoby immediately began unfastening his life vest. "I can go in after him, if you like." He was already barefoot but now took off his cap in readiness. Jasmine realised that he was waiting for her, as captain, to make the call.

Just then, a smiling Neo popped his head up from a couple of metres away.

He swam over and passed a metal casket up to her. The strangely shaped casket had two flat edges and two wavy ones. There was writing on the lid. It made her think of her mum's music box but, although mysterious, this writing wasn't in code. It just said: 'under'.

Jacoby helped Neo climb back into the boat. Jasmine noticed them exchange an intricate handshake. She knew how Jacoby loved a secret handshake. It pleased her that he had one with Neo. What a nice way to make Neo feel welcome at Pirate Academy!

"So, what do we have here?" Jacoby asked, scooching over to examine the casket.

"*Under*," he read, wrinkling his nose in puzzlement. "What do you suppose that means?"

Jasmine shrugged. "Shall we see if there's any more information inside?"

The boys waited as Jasmine unclasped the lid. Sure enough, in a waterproof compartment inside the casket was a fresh roll of paper, tied with a ribbon. Jasmine passed the scroll across to Neo.

Neo took a moment to dry his hands properly before taking the note from her, slipping off the ribbon and unrolling the scroll of paper.

"Congratulations, Barracuda Blue Crew!" he read. "Your navigation is perfect. Sail around the next rocks to a sunny bay to moor and enjoy lunch. But don't stay too long! It's a serious sail over to the islands where you'll meet up with your fellow crews this evening."

Jacoby pored over the fresh set of instructions, chatting away to Neo ten to the dozen. Jasmine watched them, thinking how, over the past few weeks, they seemed to have become good friends. Then, as she looked from Jacoby's green-blue eyes to Neo's blue-green ones, a strange thought floated through her mind. Shaking her head, she pushed the ridiculous idea away. But it floated right back, like a fish that wasn't yet ready to swim off.

CHAPTER 14
STORMY WEATHER

"I thought Oceans Bound was supposed to test us to our limits," Neo smiled, as he floated on his back in the water off the sunlit cove where they had moored for lunch.

"I know, right," Jacoby agreed, drifting beside him. "But, you see, we're a dream team. With *your* incredible diving skills and my *amazing* navigation . . ."

"Don't forget our awesome captain!" Neo said, nodding his head towards the beach where Jasmine was sitting, pen in hand, updating her Captain's Logbook.

Neo paddled closer to Jacoby. "I know you and Jasmine have been friends for a long time," he said. "So, if you do want to tell her about us being brothers, I'm totally OK with that."

"Oh, er, right," Jacoby said. "Well . . . yes . . . maybe . . . soon."

"Think it over," Neo said, lightly. "I know I was the

one who said we should take some time – and we have. Maybe this weekend is a good chance to tell her, away from the others."

Neo began swimming gracefully back to the shallows. Jacoby lingered in the same spot, thinking how lovely it would be to stay here, drifting in the warm water with the early afternoon sun sending down its rays. But he knew that they had been eased gently into Oceans Bound. Far tougher challenges lay in wait. That was a bit scary but also super exciting – it was why they were here! Feeling a flutter through his chest, he rolled over and began the swim back to shore.

***

Jasmine sat between her two crewmates in the hull, as they took another close look at the map and co-ordinates they had been given. She was excited to continue their mission.

"I reckon it's about a ninety-minute sail," Jacoby told the others, glancing back at the bay. "We could have had a longer swim."

"Better safe than sorry," Jasmine said, rolling up the map and handing it over to Jacoby. "Let's keep you on navigation. And both of you on sails for now. I'll start off helming but we can switch around so we all get a turn."

As they eased away from shore, she could feel the wind building up behind them.

"Now, we're sailing!" Jacoby announced happily, the ocean breeze ruffling his hair.

They made excellent progress and were excited to get their first glimpse of the cluster of islands in the distance. Jasmine scanned the ocean for signs of their fellow Barracudas. "I wonder how everyone else is getting on," she said. "And when we'll see them all again."

"That's easy!" Jacoby called over, grinning. "When we welcome them to *our* island! Remember, guys, bonus points for first to arrive!"

***

The storm didn't exactly come out of nowhere. All the same, there was a pretty sudden shift in the weather. The wind had been building ever since the start of their afternoon sail and had speeded them on their way. Now, suddenly, the waters were becoming more and more choppy and the small Academy yacht was tossed around in the waves.

Neo was taking his turn at the helm but, catching Jasmine's expression, immediately offered to return to sail trimming. They quickly swapped positions.

"Just let me know if you feel any signs of seasickness," Jasmine told him.

"Nothing yet," Neo assured her. "I think Nurse C's tablets are working a treat!"

As the port side of the boat tilted high up in the swells, Jacoby suddenly lost his footing. He steadied himself and straightened his cap. Which a fresh gust of wind promptly blew askew. Pulling the cap off his head, he tossed it like a frisbee into the hold.

As the boys held tight to the sail sheets, Jasmine assessed the rapidly worsening weather. Where the sky had been bright blue before, it was now a louring grey-black. The wind was getting stronger all the time and, on top of this, there was now a driving rain. And was that a crack of lightning?

They had three options, Jasmine figured. 1) Stay here and wait for the weather to change. 2) Veer off-course and try to find somewhere to shelter from the storm. Or 3) draw down deep on everything they had learnt in sailing class and keep going towards the islands. The weather looked unlikely to change any time soon. If they veered away from their course, they might not make it to the target island by nightfall. Jasmine reasoned that staying on course made the best sense.

There was no time to lose!

"Ready to gybe?" she called out.

There was no delay in her crew's response. "Yes, Captain!"

Jasmine steered the small boat across the wind, as the boys trimmed the sails. The boom pole swung sharply across the boat. The three experienced sailors ducked cleanly out of its way. Coming out of the turn, they were on a much better line with the wind.

"Nice gybing, crew!" Jasmine called, encouragingly. "Much more of that to come!"

Neo and Jacoby fell into a strong rhythm, listening out for Jasmine's commands and then pulling in, or releasing, the sail sheets – depending on the direction they were turning. The boat pitched up and down but, to his surprise, Neo didn't feel at all queasy. Instead, he was pumped with pure exhilaration at the speed they were travelling plus the satisfaction of working as a team, through the wind and rain and the rough, roiling waves.

He glanced over at Jacoby, who seemed totally in his element. Neo thought back to a couple of hours earlier when they had been floating in the tranquil waters of the cove. Jacoby had looked blissfully happy then but, if anything, he looked even happier now.

"Everything OK, guys?" Jasmine called over to them.

"Better than OK, Captain!" Jacoby shouted back. "This is what we've been training for! This is what we came here to do!" He beamed at his crewmates through the lashing rain. Behind him came another crack of lightning.

***

As Jasmine steered the boat through yet another turn, she could feel the power of the storm at last beginning to dwindle. She found herself trembling. In the thick of the storm, there had been no time for nerves. Instead they had stored themselves up and now let loose, flooding her body from her head to her toes.

Glancing ahead, she saw with relief that the sky was changing colour again – this time, thankfully, from smoke grey to pale blue.

The islands were already much closer than she had expected. As they sailed on, the wind began to drop and she realised she could no longer feel prickling raindrops on her face. The sun was breaking through again, as if to congratulate them on getting through their ordeal and welcome them to the islands.

It was now calm and dry enough for Jacoby to take

a fresh look at their map. Calm enough too for him to hand across his line of rope to Neo and move over to Jasmine's side.

"We just need to steer a little more to Starboard," Jacoby advised her. "See, there should be a channel opening up right . . . about . . . now!"

And there it was. "Great job, Captain!" Jacoby told her, moving back into position.

Steering towards the island, Jasmine let out a deep sigh. They had got through their first real Oceans Bound challenge successfully. She felt so proud of the way the three of them had pulled together as a crew. It made her feel confident about whatever was coming their way next.

CHAPTER 15
TREASURE ISLAND

"**W**e made it!" Neo said, smiling as he stepped barefoot onto the beach and spun around, taking in their beautiful island surroundings.

"More importantly," Jacoby noted, "we made it *first*!"

The pristine white-sand beach was dotted with coconut palms. Between two of these had been strung a volleyball net, clearly in preparation for the Barracudas' arrival. Neo noticed what looked like bulging bags of food attached to the top of two other palm trees.

"Fact check, *we* got here first!" boomed a familiar voice from the end of the beach. Cosmo emerged from a clearing, his arms laden with driftwood. He was striding between Shay and Ocean, who immediately raced over to Jasmine, dropping the wood she had collected on the beach and hugging her roommate.

"How did you get on out there? It was pretty brutal, right?"

Jasmine nodded, hugging Ocean tightly and waving to the others. "It's so good to see you guys!"

Cosmo and Shay added their wood to Ocean's pile. "Good to see you, Blunt," Cosmo said, in a cheeky tone. "We were wondering when you might rock up."

Jacoby narrowed his eyes. "You can't have been here that much earlier than us, Cosmo. Besides, there's no shame in coming second."

Cosmo and Shay glanced back towards the clearing. Now Ari, Layla and Rose appeared, all carrying fishing lines and nets. They were just ahead of Kaz, Carmen and Fergus, who had baskets of fruit and vegetables.

"Just so we're clear, Jacoby, you were the *fourth* crew to arrive," Cosmo told him, grinning widely. "We're just waiting on Crew Leif now."

"I don't understand," Jacoby said. "Where are all your boats moored?"

"There's a sheltered harbour around the West side of the island. You might want to relocate your boat there later. Want to have a look around?"

Jacoby nodded, turning back to Neo. "Wanna come?"

Neo shook his head. "I'm going to help the others get the fire started and then maybe get to work on collecting whatever food is waiting up there in the palms."

"Oh, OK," Jacoby said, wondering if maybe he should stay too.

"Catch you later, Neo!" Cosmo boomed, throwing his arm around Jacoby's shoulder and leading him away to the edge of the beach. "All joking aside," Cosmo said, "it's good to see you. That was some fairly dicey sailing this afternoon, right?"

"It was," Jacoby agreed. "But when you have someone like Jasmine as your captain, you have nothing to fear. She is one hundred per cent across everything!"

"Quite," Cosmo said. "Quite! Same with Ocean. And the diving challenge ... Of course, Shay made light work of that!"

Jacoby beamed. "Neo did a brilliant *free* dive." He could tell *that* had got Cosmo's attention.

Cosmo nodded, thoughtfully. "Things got a bit hair-raising for Kaz and co out there, you know? They got pushed way off track. Ari's boat went over to help them out. Barracuda to Barracuda, as it were."

That was interesting – and also worrying. Jacoby didn't like to think of anything bad happening to any of his classmates. They were all in this together.

"Oh, look!" Cosmo pointed out to the water. "Our

fifth and final crew is about to moor up." He waved. "Over here, Leif! Great to see you guys!" Under his breath, he added, "At last!"

Leif, Wing and Lewis all waved from their yacht as they dropped anchor.

"Well, that's all of us," Cosmo said. "All Barracudas made it through Day One in one piece!"

Jacoby knew his friend was given to drama and exaggeration but, all the same, he shivered. Was there a scenario in which all the Barracudas might *not* have made it through Day One?

***

On the beach, the driftwood fire was blazing away. Close by, Jasmine was sorting through the first bag of supplies that had been retrieved from the palm trees, while Ocean and Shay were currently at the top of the other tree, fetching down the second food parcel. Meanwhile, Neo was busy sorting through the haul from the fishing nets.

A game of volleyball was underway, with Ari's crew taking on Kaz's. Ari might have come to Kaz's rescue out at sea, but she and her crew were showing Crew Kaz no mercy on the volleyball court.

Everyone stopped what they were doing to greet the

final crew with cheers. Leif, Wing and Lewis gamely waved as they took in their island surroundings with wide eyes. Fergus raced over to give his twin brother a bear hug.

"Hey," Ocean called from the top of the palm. "Do you guys have the missing piece of our jigsaw?" Met by puzzled looks, she explained. "The casket you dived for. Do you have it?"

"Right here!" Leif said, holding it up into the sunlight.

"Great!" Ocean said, pointing to a spot beyond the fire where the other crews had placed together the caskets they had dived for. Leif strode over, followed closely by Jacoby and Wing, and all the other Barracudas. Ocean and Shay shinned back down the tree with the second bag of food.

As he drew closer, Jacoby saw what Ocean meant by a 'jigsaw piece'. The caskets all joined up like jigsaw pieces, their wavy sides meeting wavy sides. There was writing on all five caskets and now, as Leif inserted the final casket, the message was crystal clear. Indeed, as the five caskets snapped together, the words were suddenly lit up in bright aqua light:

Never underestimate a Barracuda!

Jacoby grinned. He should have known the moment he'd seen the word 'under' on their own casket. He felt very proud that the teachers had used the motto *he* had come up with!

There were cheers as Leif stepped back completing the jigsaw. Then the group began to chant . . .

Never underestimate a Barracuda!
Never underestimate a Barracuda!
Never underestimate a Barracuda!

They hugged each other and jumped up and down on the sand. Totally unaware that, all this time, they were being closely watched.

CHAPTER 16
THE WATCHERS

On the neighbouring island, Reef Lermentov and his two good friends from Stingray Class, Harper and Antoni, were passing a pair of high-range binoculars back and forth between them. As was Academy tradition, the three older students had been given the honour of sailing one step ahead of the Barracudas and laying the trail for Oceans Bound weekend. Reef, Harper and Antoni had had a long and busy day, setting up the morning diving challenges and then preparing the island welcome for the Barracudas.

Now their work was done for the day, the three Stingrays were enjoying a well-earnt break, cooking up their dinner on a barbecue which they had set up on a grassy outcrop facing out to sea.

"Did you see my sister scale that tree?" Reef asked his friends, proudly.

"Yes, Reef," Harper said. "Ocean did great. We all

know she's the true superstar of the Lermentov clan." There was a cheeky smile on her face as she passed over the binoculars.

"Very funny," Reef said, not looking at all amused. He was as proud of Ocean as he was fond of her, but he didn't enjoy the two of them being compared. Especially when his whip-smart, agile, sailing-sensation of a sister was a whole two years younger than him!

"Sharkmeat hot dogs are ready when you are," Antoni called over from the barbecue. "And I've made some spicy bush-tomato relish, just because."

"Antoni, you are quite the chef!" Harper said, impressed. "I am ravenous! When the Commodore and Mayday briefed us on Oceans Bound, I didn't realise just how much work it would be getting everything set up ahead of the Barracudas."

"Well, we've got a busy day ahead of us tomorrow too," Reef said. "So let's eat up and get a good night's rest so we can be up early, laying out the next part of their course." He gazed towards the line of five coloured bottles, which awaited fresh instruction scrolls.

"Sounds like a plan!" Harper agreed, sipping from a freshly shucked coconut. "Oh, that is sooo yummy!"

"Come on, tuck in!" Antoni passed each of them a plate piled high with food.

As they devoured their delicious dinner, the three longtime friends from Stingray Class talked and joked about their memories of their own Oceans Bound expedition, two years earlier. They were totally unaware that, as they chatted away and nibbled on their tasty shark hot dogs, they too were being watched.

CHAPTER 17
THE GAME CHANGES

"**W**hat's that rustling?" Antoni asked, turning to scan the dark undergrowth behind them.

"Probably just a wild boar," Harper said, grinning. "Just think how many sausages we could make if we caught it!"

At the sound of fresh movement behind them, Reef jumped to his feet, dropped his empty plate and reached for the sword he had placed close by his chair.

Harper laughed, lightly. "Reef Lermentov, are you preparing to joust with a boar?" Her eyes shimmered bright in the starlight. "This is the stuff of Academy legend!"

The smile froze on her lips, however, as four hooded figures stepped out of the bushes to join the three Stingray students on the grassy ledge. The newcomers all wore masks, fashioned after traditional ships' figureheads. The starlight illuminated the strangely thin eyebrows, pouting mouths and rosy cheeks. Each of them brandished their own sword.

Still, Reef was not ready to back down. He gestured for Harper and Antoni to retrieve their own weapons, before calmly addressing the masked agents. "We know who you are . . . Agents of the despicable League of True Pirates. You have no business here. I suggest you leave this island before things get unpleasant." Glancing across at his classmates, who both now clasped their swords, he added, "We have been trained by the best."

There was a moment of stand-off, during which nobody moved or spoke. Then, the second tallest of the four agents of the league raised his free hand and lifted his mask over the top of his head. Noah Ripley stood grinning at the three Stingrays before him.

"Well, honestly, kids, this is no less impressive than I might have expected. But, face facts, you are outnumbered and outclassed. You may be highly-trained pirate *apprentices*. But we are *actual* pirates, who have each killed, on more than one occasion."

As Ripley finished speaking, Reef leapt forwards, sword outstretched. Ripley lifted his own weapon to parry it and they began fighting in close combat.

Meanwhile, Harper and Antoni faced up to the three remaining agents. They had both been expertly coached by Captain Molina, but would it prove sufficient to defeat three formidable foes between them?

It would not. Five minutes later, all three pirate apprentices found themselves bound in intricate ropes from their shoulders to their feet. The LOT P agents had taken the young pirates' weapons and placed them tantalisingly out of reach, then tied their three helpless prisoners to the tallest tree in the clearing – a sturdy Norfolk pine.

"You won't get away with this," Reef snapped, as the agents began retreating back towards the thick undergrowth.

Noah Ripley smiled. "Thanks for your input," he said. "But I suspect we will." Stepping forwards, he lifted Reef's pair of binoculars from the grass. Bringing them to his face, he looked across the water to the beach opposite, where the Barracudas were now clustered around their blazing campfire, singing sea shanties, accompanied by Neo on his ukulele.

"The Barracudas seem to be having a wonderful time over there, don't they?" Noah drew down the binoculars and smiled. "If only they knew, the rules of the game have now changed. Indeed, it might be truer to say that the game itself has changed. And, for some of our favourite Barracudas, things are about to get a whole lot more . . . interesting."

CHAPTER 18
SNAKES

Neo felt his nose tickled by the morning sun and opened his eyes to the new day. Some of the Barracudas had camped on the island overnight, but Neo and his crew had chosen to sleep on their boat. It had been such a warm night, he and Jacoby had brought their sleeping bags out onto the deck to sleep under the stars. The fact he had slept so well on the water was another sure sign that Nurse Carmichael's magic pills were working! Feeling light and happy, he moved over to the edge of the boat to look back across at the beach.

A line of coloured bottles – gleaming like jewels in the morning sun – had been planted on the sand. Neo felt a bubbling sense of excitement about what adventures lay in store today. His classmates had been talking around the fire last night and everyone agreed that, from what they'd heard, the challenges on Day Two of Oceans Bound were likely to be *much* tougher than those on Day One. Neo smiled. *Bring it!*

"Morning!" Jacoby exclaimed, jerking suddenly to life. Spotting the row of bottles on the sand, a grin spread across his face. "Are we the first crew up?"

Neo nodded. "I think so."

"Well then," Jacoby said, his eyes sparkling. "How about I swim over and collect the blue bottle? We can make an early start on our next mission!"

Jasmine popped her head up from the hold, already washed and dressed. "We said we'd all have breakfast together this morning, remember?"

"I know," Jacoby said. "But how about we change our plan and get ahead of the others? Remember, bonus points for—"

Jasmine shook her head. "Jacoby, you do know that bonus points are awarded for all kinds of achievements, not just racing to get everywhere first!"

Jacoby was undeterred. "True, true," he said. "But it can't hurt, can it?" He had already stripped down to his shorts and was ready to dive.

Neo caught Jasmine's amused expression and shook his head.

"All right," she said. "I suppose it can't hurt."

Jacoby beamed. "I won't be long!" he told them. "And I can treat the swim as my morning wash!"

He splashed down into the water.

***

Twenty minutes later, the three of them were sitting in the hold, all dressed in their sailing uniforms and studying their next set of directions, taken from the blue bottle. Glancing back at the beach, Neo was pleased to see the four other coloured bottles remained untouched.

"This looks clear to me," Jasmine said, studying the scroll. "We sail in a north-east direction around to one of the largest islands in this group."

Jacoby tapped the map. "And we look out for a lighthouse!" he said.

Moments later, they were speeding away from the beach. Glancing back over his shoulder, Neo noticed that Cosmo, Shay and Ocean had finally found their way to the line of coloured bottles. Cosmo began pointing in Neo's direction, shaking his head and shouting. Neo could imagine the kinds of words tumbling from Cosmo's mouth. He gave his baffled classmates a cheeky wave, then turned back to the sail sheets.

***

It wasn't long before they arrived at their destination. At first glance, this island looked far less welcoming than the one they had left behind earlier. Here, there were no lush coconut palms lining the sandy shore. Instead, a mean strip of beach soon gave way to jagged cliffs, to which clung some of the most sun-baked and spindly plants Neo had seen in his life. The whole island had an air of dryness and decay – as if no one had set foot here in many years.

"Let's drop anchor here!" Jasmine's voice drew Neo's attention.

"I can barely see the lighthouse!" Jacoby said, straining his neck to gaze up the cliffs. "Oh, there it is! But how do we get up there? Will we need to scale the cliff face by rope?"

Neo noticed something over on the sand – it looked like words made up of small stones and shells. "I think there's a message for us over there," he told the others.

"Great!" Jasmine said. "Let's swim over and see."

"Everyone got water, hats and sunscreen?" Jacoby asked. "Because it looks like we're going to need them this morning!" They all checked their waterproof kit bags, then clipped them shut and lowered them into the water. Then, the three of them jumped down into the water themselves and started swimming, side by side, towards the beach.

"Wait!" Jasmine called out. "Did anyone pack the first-aid kit? Just in case."

"In my kit bag!" Jacoby called back, swimming on to shore.

Neo had been right. There was a message waiting for them on the sand, neatly composed of stones and shells:

Welcome to Spider Island!
This way to the lighthouse . . .

"Spider Island?!" Jacoby said, suddenly sounding rather nervous. "When they say *Spider . . .*"

Neo shot his brother a reassuring look, then returned to the message on the sand. Beneath the words was an arrow, made of smaller stones, pointing towards the jagged cliff. Stepping forwards, Neo now saw that there was a steep path cutting up through the rock. He suspected they were in for a tough climb, made even tougher by the strong heat of the sun.

He suddenly felt Jasmine's hand clamp tight onto his arm. "Careful, Neo! Stay very still!"

At once, Neo froze, knowing from her voice that something was really wrong. Now, Jasmine nodded slowly in the direction of the stone and shell message. A snake had slithered its way between the letters and paused in the middle to raise its head towards them.

"Is that a Rainbow Swordhead?" Jasmine asked, her voice low and husky.

"I think it might be," Jacoby said brightly, sounding more curious than afraid.

Neo gazed at the snake. As it reared up dead straight, the reptile looked like a lethal, albeit very colourful, weapon.

Jasmine spoke slowly. "The Rainbow Swordhead is a highly venomous pit viper. And I doubt this is the only one on this island. There's likely to be a snake pit near here, full of them."

Neo shuddered at the thought. "You seem to know an awful lot about snakes," he said.

"When you have as bad *ophidophobia* as Jasmine," Jacoby said, "it pays to be an expert! In case you don't know, *ophidophobia* means . . ."

"Yes," Neo said, "I get it." He tried to channel some of his brother's relaxed attitude. He felt relieved as the snake lowered itself back down again, but his nerves swiftly returned as the Rainbow Swordhead began slithering directly towards them.

Or rather, to be totally accurate, the snake started slithering *straight towards Neo!*

CHAPTER 19
SPIDERS

"**K**eep very, *very* still," Jasmine told Neo.

"Try not to panic!" Jacoby added, not very helpfully.

Neo kept his feet rooted to the spot and did his best to keep his legs from shaking. He couldn't bear to watch as the snake's head reached his toes. He could feel the surprising weight of the reptile as its long body slid slowly over his thin deck shoes. Neo held his breath and tried to zone out.

At last, he felt Jasmine squeeze his shoulder. "It's OK now." Turning, he saw the snake had propelled itself into the shallows. Jasmine might feel reassured, but now Neo was even more worried.

"I didn't know snakes could swim!"

Jasmine nodded. "The Rainbow Swordhead is equally at home in the water as on dry land," she said, as if reading aloud from a school textbook.

Neo's mouth hung agape. "So you're saying that . . . later . . . when we swim back to the boat . . . we'll be sharing the water with . . ." His mouth was now so dry, he couldn't get the words out.

"Possibly!" Jacoby said, cutting in, brightly. "But, hey, let's not worry about that for now."

Neo frowned. "I disagree. This totally feels like something we should worry about *right now*."

"Think about it," Jacoby said. "Why would the Commodore and Captain Salt send us here if there was a problem? Oceans Bound is designed to challenge us, not to send us into the path of real danger!" He strode off towards the cliff path, squishing down his sun hat and looking every bit the intrepid explorer. "Come on, guys! Any further delay and we lose our lead over the other crews!"

Neo's eyes met Jasmine's. She shrugged. They followed Jacoby onto the path. The challenging climb to the lighthouse might prove a very useful distraction.

***

"It's official! I've lost half my body weight in sweat!" Jacoby announced, coming to a stop on the dusty path. He reached for his water bottle, but it was already empty.

Neo passed over his own bottle, encouraging Jacoby to top up his rations.

"I thought as we climbed higher, we might get a glimpse of some of the other crews," Jasmine said, pausing on the track to gaze out to sea.

Neo stood beside her, also scanning the shimmering turquoise waters. "Can't see any sign of them. They must have been sent to different islands."

"Perhaps," Jacoby said. "But remember, guys, we got a super early start on them!"

"True," Jasmine agreed. "OK, crew . . . ready for part two of the climb?"

The second half of the climb was far tougher than the first. They were now more exposed to the sun's glare. Neo could feel sweat dripping down his forehead and ears, even under his sun hat. He was starting to feel a bit giddy. It had probably been a mistake to skip breakfast. Suddenly he felt hand on his arm.

"We've got this!" Jacoby told him. "Not far now!"

His brother's encouraging words were just what Neo needed to keep going.

***

At last, they reached the summit. And there, in all its glory, was the lighthouse. Only, in truth, the lighthouse was far from a glorious sight. In fact, it wasn't far off being an utter ruin. As the three young explorers approached, the shadow of the tall structure fell over them. It gave them a brief respite from the searing heat.

Gazing up, they could see that there was no lamp turning up above. The domed roof was broken in several places and there was tell-tale rubble sprinkled all around the base.

"Is it even stable?" Jasmine wondered aloud.

"Only one way to find out!" Jacoby said, striding on towards the faded and peeling red paint of the main door.

Neo and Jasmine were left standing outside. Neo frowned. "Under any normal circs, I'd say let's give it a wide berth. But I guess Jacoby's right – the Commodore and Captain Salt wouldn't set us this challenge if it wasn't safe?"

Jasmine nodded. "Agreed. And the sooner we go in and collect whatever clue is waiting for us, the sooner we can be on our way and leave Spider Island far behind!"

"It's really not a very nice place, is it?" Neo said.

"It's horrible!" Jasmine grinned, taking another sip of water.

The two friends walked up to the doorway together and followed Jacoby inside. The scene that met them was a strange one indeed.

The inside of the lighthouse was silvery-white, cool and dank. It was like walking into a thick mist or the centre of a cloud. It made it hard to get a grip on their new surroundings. But as Neo and Jasmine forged onwards, they began to make sense of it. In the centre of the lighthouse was a tall spiral staircase. In all likelihood, this led directly up to the lamp-room.

It was impossible to tell because the entire metal structure was covered with the thickest spider webs Neo had ever seen in his life. Shafts of light, breaking in through the shattered roof, wove through the thick webs, lighting them from within. Moving closer, Neo could see the plump spiders, lounging at the centre of their creation, seeming proud of their work.

Neo turned to Jasmine, in wonder. "I have never seen anything like this!"

"Me neither!" Jasmine replied, shaking her head slowly.

"How many spiders do you think there *are* in here?" Neo wondered, reaching out a finger to gently prod one of the webs. "A few hundred? A thousand?"

Jasmine shrugged. "It's like they've entirely taken the place over."

Neo wasn't really frightened of spiders. Still, there was something unsettling about the unusual thickness of these webs and the presence of quite so many spiders. Everyone knew that a spider had eight eyes. Multiply that by a few hundred (at least) and that came to a very large number of eyes, all watching the newcomers with interest. It really did feel as if the island belonged to the spiders and the three young humans were only their guests. Neo shuddered. Then he was possessed by a horrible new fear.

"Jasmine, where's Jacoby?"

CHAPTER 20
A LOT MORE SPIDERS

Jasmine's eyes met Neo's. She could see her own worry reflected in her friend's face.

Just then, there was a noise from above. It sounded like someone falling heavily. It was followed by a low moan.

"Jacoby!" Neo cried, his feet already on the stairs.

"Wait!" Jasmine shot out her hand. "Neo, we don't know what's going on here yet!"

"Exactly!" Neo shot back. "And I'm not waiting down here to find out. I seem to remember being told that Barracudas always look out for one another." He began bounding up the web-laden stairway.

Jasmine flushed with burning embarrassment. She didn't mean that they *shouldn't* go and rescue Jacoby, only that they should take a moment to devise a failsafe plan. In Leadership lessons at the Academy, the Commodore often talked about the importance of the decisions you make in a split-second in the heart of danger and uncertainty.

She stood at the foot of the staircase, weighing up what to do next. This time, Jasmine listened to the call of her pounding heart, not her cool head. She raced up the stairs to join the others. Whatever fresh danger was waiting up there, they would face it together!

It was like running through an ice tunnel. The webs got thicker as the stairway circled up the lighthouse. She didn't have time to be afraid. Besides, they were spiders. If they had been snakes, it would have been another story. Then Jasmine thought of Jacoby. He had correctly identified that she had *ophidophobia* – an extreme fear of snakes. But it was just as true that Jacoby had *arachnophobia* – an overwhelming fear of spiders. It would have taken an unbelievable amount of bravery for him to even step foot onto the stairs.

Now, Jasmine reached the top of the stairway and found herself inside the lamp-room. Neo was close by, standing up on a ledge. Jacoby was farther away, in the centre of the room, frozen to the spot. And it wasn't hard to see why.

The entire lamp-room had been taken over by spiders. There was no visible floor here. Instead, it was a moving carpet of spiders – even bigger, hairier spiders than the ones lounging in their webs on the stairwell. And the spiders weren't only on the floor. Glancing up at the broken ceiling, Jasmine saw that there were hundreds more spiders suspended from the rafters. It was all of Jacoby's worst nightmares come to horrible life.

"Jacoby!" she heard Neo say. "You don't need to do this. Let me take over now."

Jacoby seemed unable to speak. He moved his head and, following his gaze, Jasmine saw where he was looking. Just beyond the centre of the room, where the lighthouse lamp stood broken and still, was a blue glass bottle, with a scroll of paper inside it. The problem was that between Jacoby and the all-important bottle was the moving sea of spiders. What had the Commodore's team been thinking, placing their next instructions here?

"Neo's right," Jasmine called out now. "You've been beyond brave, Jacoby. But please let us take over now. We're a team."

It was as if he didn't hear her. As if he was locked in a world of his own. He drew a deep breath in then out, then took another step closer to the bottle.

"Amazing move, buddy!" Neo called out, encouragingly. "You're almost there now. Just keep moving, at your own pace."

Jasmine was surprised by Neo's approach. But she realised that Neo was incredibly smart. By being so patient and talking so encouragingly, he was giving Jacoby an amazing chance to face one of his deepest, darkest fears. And it seemed to be working! Jacoby appeared to be in a trance, but Jasmine realised that he was moving in the right direction, carefully placing his feet so as not to harm any spiders.

"That's it, Jacoby! Just another couple of careful steps!"

Jasmine glanced across at Neo, smiling and giving him a thumbs-up. She was relieved when he smiled back, warmly. No hard feelings then.

"It's almost in your reach now," Neo told Jacoby. "Just one more—"

Before Neo could finish, Jacoby had taken that next step and was able to simply reach down and take the blue bottle in his hand. As he did so, he sighed.

"You're a superstar!" Neo called.

"This is your bravest moment ever!" Jasmine told him, proud of her friend.

There was the flicker of a smile on Jacoby's face, but then he seemed to notice once more the number of spiders between him and safety. He began to tremble.

"You've totally got this!" Neo told him, in the same, supportive tone. "Now start walking back to me. Come on, Jacoby, just one foot in front of the other!"

Jasmine let out a sigh of relief as he began moving again. Neo continued to guide him back, in the same calm, upbeat voice. He couldn't have given his friend stronger support if he had magically extended his arm all the way across the room and pulled him back.

Jacoby took his time but, at last, he had made it back to where Neo was standing. Now Neo did reach out a hand and helped Jacoby up onto the ledge to join him. He took the bottle out of Jacoby's quivering fingers and passed it over to Jasmine. She watched as Neo drew Jacoby into a hug and told him, "I'm so proud of you, brother. So, *so* proud!"

Jasmine froze. Did Neo just say *brother*? Staring at Neo's blue-green eyes, Jasmine found herself begin to tremble. She had to grip the blue glass bottle more tightly so that she didn't drop it. Now she looked over at Jacoby's green-blue eyes, and shook her head slowly. Suddenly, everything felt strange and new.

She observed the two of them carefully. They were so very different in so many ways. And yet, from the first time she had seen Neo, she had felt there was something deeply familiar about him. And now she knew why. It wasn't only the colour of their eyes. There was something about the way they moved and held themselves.

Now Jasmine had seen it, she couldn't *unsee* it. Neo and Jacoby were brothers. How long had the two of them been keeping this massive secret?

CHAPTER 21
SHARKS

A fireworks display was exploding inside Jacoby's belly. He had done it! He, Jacoby Blunt, had done something off-the-scale brave. Standing beside Neo, he glanced back across the floor of moving spiders. His tummy instantly clenched. But, as he kept on looking, something really strange happened. The fear he had felt before began to soften – like a knot untying itself. Thinking about how he had bravely made his way through the seething mass of deadly spiders to retrieve their all-important instructions, he felt waves of calm and pride flooding his mind and body. It was as if he'd grown a metre taller.

He turned back to Neo, expecting to see a smile on his brother's face. But Neo wasn't smiling. In fact, he looked worried.

"Hey, what's wrong? We got the bottle! I looked my fear squarely in the eye and I said—"

Neo nodded. "Yes, you did great!"

Jacoby's eyes narrowed, sensing that a major 'but' was about to arrive. Neo reached out carefully to take hold of Jacoby's left wrist.

"I think one of the spiders bit you," Neo said. "Perhaps when you reached over to take the bottle. Take a look."

Jacoby saw the tell-tale red lump, with two tiny puncture wounds, on the back of his left hand. It wasn't very big. And it didn't hurt. In fact, he could barely feel it.

"I feel fine," Jacoby assured Neo. "Actually, I feel amazing!"

Jasmine had joined the boys. She inspected Jacoby's wound carefully, then looked up again. "Sometimes it takes a few minutes for a spider bite to have an effect," she said. "You should be fine once we inject you with anti-venom from the first-aid kit. It's in your kit bag, right?"

They had all left their bags down at the lighthouse door. They made their way back down the web-covered stairwell, watched by the lounging spiders. Jasmine clutched the prized bottle in her hands. Jacoby felt elated from his recent triumph. But, now his adrenaline levels were settling, he could feel a distinct throbbing coming from the spider bite.

"Do either of you happen to know what breed of spiders these are?" he enquired, casually.

"Sorry," Neo said. "Spiders aren't my specialist subject."

Jasmine shook her head also. "Don't worry, Jacoby. Our anti-venom is good for about ninety per cent of spiders' bites."

Jacoby gulped. Ninety per cent was great, obviously, but what if his bite was from one of the remaining ten per cent of spiders? Was it his imagination or was the throbbing now getting stronger? He glanced down at his hand and was fairly sure the red lump had swelled to double its original size. Still, no problem! The anti-venom would sort things out in a jiffy.

Reaching the lighthouse door, they grabbed their bags and stumbled back outside. The sudden blast of light and heat was a shock to their senses. There was a stone bench outside the lighthouse. Jacoby hadn't noticed it on the way in. He followed the others over to it.

"Are you OK if I go into your bag and get the first-aid kit?" Jasmine asked.

Jacoby nodded, grateful for her help. "You know I have no secrets!" he said with a grin.

Jasmine gave him a rather strange look, then began riffling through his kit bag.

"Here," Neo said, reaching for Jacoby's hand again. "Let me take another look. Buddy, I don't want to alarm you, but I think it's getting bigger and more inflamed."

Jacoby nodded. "I agree. But it's a bit soon to start panicking, right?"

"Definitely," Neo said. "One application of the anti-venom and you'll be right as rain."

"It's not in here!" Jasmine cried out. "Jacoby, are you sure you packed the first-aid kit?"

Now Jacoby allowed himself a blast of panic. Because it was actually quite possible that, in his eagerness to get on with their mission, he *might* have left the first-aid kit on the boat.

"I think I, erm . . . must have left it on the boat!"

"Jacoby!" Jasmine exclaimed, crossly. "You have to be more careful! This isn't a game."

"OK, Jasmine," Neo said. "Take it easy. We all make mistakes."

Now Jasmine looked upset. "I'm sorry, Jacoby. I didn't mean to snap. I think everything is just getting to me . . . the snakes, the spiders, the heat . . . And I'm *really* worried about you. That bite looks painful."

Jacoby smiled up at her, sheltering his eyes from the sun. "It looks worse than it feels," he said. It wasn't true but he thought it was probably what she needed to hear.

"All right then," Jasmine said. "I guess we head back down the cliff path to the shore, get back on the boat ASAP and apply the anti-venom there."

"Good plan!" Neo agreed.

Jacoby clipped his kit bag shut and slung it over his shoulder. Then he noticed the glass bottle in Jasmine's hand. "Shall we read our next instructions before we set off?"

Jasmine nodded, passing him the note. "I think *you* should do the honours."

"Now let's see," he said, smoothing out the tightly rolled paper on the bench. Suddenly, a chill passed through him. Was this a side effect of his bite? Taking a steadying breath, he looked at the note in his hands, hoping that the info about the next part of their mission would be a pleasing distraction. Unfortunately, it wasn't.

"What does it say?" Neo asked.

"Congratulations, Barracudas!" Jacoby read. "Now you know why they call this place Spider Island. But what are you going to do about the sharks?"

"Sharks!" Jasmine and Neo responded in unison.

"Well, that's what it—" Jacoby began. But the others had already begun running over to the top of the cliff path. Jacoby followed, clutching the note in one hand and feeling his other hand growing heavier and hotter from the spider bite.

He joined his crewmates at the edge of the cliff. From here, they had a clear view of the thin strip of beach and the ocean beyond. They all looked down to the turquoise waters below. There was their small boat – with the first-aid kit on board – moored a short distance from shore. And there, between the shore and the boat, was an ominous line of shark fins.

CHAPTER 22
THE MYSTERY OF THE MISSING CREW

In tranquil turquoise waters, over on the other side of the chain of islands, two sleek yachts sailed carefully towards each other. The boats' young captains steered their vessels expertly, coming to a stop side by side in the shimmering waters.

"How's it going, guys?" Ocean called out across the water.

"At the risk of sounding boastful, we are smashing this course!" Leif said, letting go of the steering wheel and leaning back to give his arms and shoulders a relaxing stretch.

"Us too!" Cosmo boomed. "We've completed our first two tasks and we're on our way to number three." To prove his point, he held up two empty purple bottles.

On the neighbouring boat, Wing lifted two green bottles. "Level pegging," he declared.

"Have you seen much of the other crews, Leif?" Ocean asked her fellow captain.

Leif nodded. "We were sailing close by Ari, Layla and Rose, this morning," he told her. "Our dive spots were fairly near to each other. How about you guys?"

"We sailed past Kaz, Fergus and Carmen mid-morning," Ocean replied. "They were in the middle of doing their dive challenge." Ocean smiled across at Lewis. "Fergus took the dive! He was stoked!"

Lewis grinned. He always liked hearing how his twin brother was getting on.

Ocean saw Wing move closer to Leif. "Has anyone seen Jasmine's boat?" Wing now asked.

Shay shook their head. "Not since first thing this morning."

"When they slipped away before the rest of us had breakfast," Cosmo couldn't resist adding. "Extremely bad form!"

Ocean frowned. "Guys, I'm starting to get worried."

"Do you think something might have happened to them?" Leif asked.

Ocean's eyes met Leif's across the water. "Don't you think it's strange the rest of our boats have been criss-crossing each other's courses all day, but neither your crew nor mine have seen a trace of Jasmine's boat since first light?"

Leif nodded, thoughtfully. "Are you really concerned, Ocean? To the point where you feel we should call off the afternoon's task and raise the emergency alarm?"

"And risk Oceans Bound being abandoned?" Cosmo cut in. "Absolutely not!"

Leif exchanged a glance with his own crew, before turning back to Ocean. "If you're really worried, then we should consider all options. Barracudas always look out for each other."

Cosmo shook his head. "You're forgetting that we watched them slink away this morning. Shay and I saw the cheeky expression on Neo's face. It's clear Neo and Jacoby hatched a plan to put one over the rest of us." He frowned. "Jas won't have been keen, of course, but they'll have overruled her."

Shay shook their head. "Jasmine isn't so easily overruled."

Leif's kind eyes sought out Ocean's again. "What do you think? Time for the flares?"

Ocean frowned, weighing her options. "No, no I guess it's too soon for that. But can we make it our mission for the rest of the day's sailing to keep a look out for them?"

"Definitely!" Leif agreed. Behind him, Wing and Lewis both nodded.

Ocean let out a sigh of relief. It felt good to have a plan in place.

The crews of the two boats made ready to sail off towards their next missions. On Ocean's boat, Shay and Cosmo took their positions on the sailing sheets. Meanwhile, across the water, Leif moved away from the wheel to allow Wing to take over the helm.

Leif leant across the edge of his boat to bump Ocean's fist. "Try not to worry," Leif told his friend. "I'm sure there's a simple explanation."

Lewis looped his arm around Leif's shoulder and grinned. "I promise you, Ocean, we'll all be having a laugh about the mystery of the missing crew tonight!"

At last, Ocean managed a smile. "I hope so," she said, getting ready to sail away.

CHAPTER 23
PRISONERS

Meanwhile, back on another island in the very same Archipelago, Ocean's older brother Reef and his two friends from Stingray Class were still tied up in rope, binding them tightly to the trunk of a tall Norfolk Pine tree. At least the tree's thick branches offered them shade from the fierce midday sun. It was now seventeen and a half hours since their capture by Noah Ripley and his LOT P accomplices, and every attempt to slip their bindings had ended in crushing defeat.

"You know the worst thing about this situation?" Reef asked his friends, gloomily.

"The fact we watched LOT P sail off with our boat, leaving us stranded here?" offered Harper. "And they made off with our emergency flares!"

"The fact I'm feeling really thirsty and hungry and badly in need of a wee," Antoni shared.

"That's *three* things, Antoni," Harper said. "But they are all valid and I can totally relate."

"All great observations, guys," Reef told his friends. "But I think the very worst thing about being tied up here all night and half the day, is we don't know what havoc Noah Ripley and the League have now caused with Oceans Bound. I'm *really* worried for the Barracudas."

Harper nodded. It was only a small nod, because she was so tightly tied to the tree. "I know it might seem worse for you, Reef – because your sister's a Barracuda – but we feel just the same. If LOT P has done harm to just one of those kids, there's going to be hell to pay!"

Reef was grateful for Harper's support but there was absolutely nothing they could do to help so long as they were tied up here.

"Ohhhh!" Antoni moaned.

"What's wrong?" Reef and Harper asked together, anxiously.

"I just thought of a *bonus* worst thing," Antoni told them. "What's Captain Quivers going to say when she hears we were unable to untie ourselves from this knotting system? It's so *embarrassing* after everything she's taught us. I've always had top marks in Knots Class."

Harper laughed, lightly. "How about we worry about

Quivers when we get back to the Academy? For now, we have to stay positive and focused." She swivelled her head around so her eyes met Reef's. "I know we're pretty sure this *is* a deserted island, so screaming is probably a total waste of our precious energy, but should we maybe try one more time?"

"Why not?" Reef agreed. "It must be a half hour since our last group scream. On the count of three, then. Three . . . two . . ."

All three opened their mouths wide. Just as they did so, they heard the sound of rustling in the undergrowth. They not only paused their screams but all held their breaths.

They were rewarded by the sound of footsteps and grunting. It was, Reef thought, perhaps the most beautiful sound he had ever heard.

A woman pushed through the foliage and appeared in the clearing, followed by a baby boar. It was, Harper thought, perhaps the most beautiful sight she had ever seen.

"Well, well, well. What have we here?" the woman enquired in a deep, throaty voice.

The woman had thick coils of braided hair, in an array of colours from sherbet pink, through deep purple to vivid orange and silver. She was dressed in a weather-beaten leather vest, which exposed her tanned, muscled arms, inked with many tattoos. She wore a vast hooped skirt. The small, snuffling boar bashed into her ankles.

"Careful, Pickle!" the woman declared, scooping him up into her arms.

Reef cleared his throat loudly. "We figured this island was deserted, Madam," he told her. "I have to say it's quite a relief to find this isn't the case."

The woman frowned at his words and tilted her head to one side. "Deserted?" she said. "You mean you tied *yourselves* up in these intricate knots?"

"No," Harper cut in. "Last night, we were attacked by agents of the League of True Pirates. They tied us up and stole our boat. We're from Pirate Academy. We're running an Oceans Bound weekend for some of the younger students."

The woman nodded. "That makes more sense! I know all about the Academy, of course, but I know nothing of this League of . . ."

"True Pirates!" Reef burst out. "We can fill you in. But maybe first you could free us?"

The woman smiled, revealing a mouth containing

only a few regular teeth. The rest were fashioned from gold, diamonds and one lone ruby. They twinkled in the sunlight. "You're making a rather large assumption that you are not my prisoners," she told Reef, producing a sword from a holster secured to her belt.

As the tip of her sword sliced through the air, close to Reef's face, he tried to calm his breath. He failed. "Are we . . . in fact . . . your prisoners?"

The woman smiled again and jumped back, then lifted her sword high and prepared to strike.

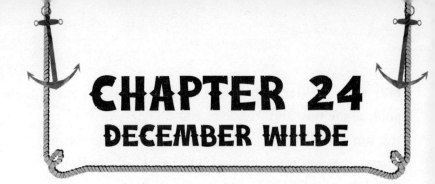

CHAPTER 24
DECEMBER WILDE

The sword sliced through the air millimetres from Reef's neck. He shut his eyes tight, fearing the worst. He thought of Ocean and how he had not only let *her* down but his parents also, and all the Lermentovs who had come before them, not to mention the Academy *and* the Pirate Federation . . .

But suddenly, he realised that he was not wounded nor dead. He was, in fact, free. Opening his eyes again, he watched the woman neatly slice through his friends' remaining ties.

"You're not my prisoners," the woman told them. "Frankly, I'm grateful for fresh company. It can get lonely on an island, with just a little boar who isn't well versed in the art of conversation." She smiled. "Welcome to my humble home. The name's December Wilde."

At this, Harper first gasped, then dropped into a deep bow. "Captain Wilde!" she declared, giddily.

"What an incredible honour to even breathe the same air as you!"

"You've heard of her?" Reef hissed.

"You haven't?" Harper hissed back. "Captain December Wilde is a true-blue pirate legend."

Overhearing this, Captain Wilde chuckled throatily. "I'll take that. Pirate legend!" She paused. "Though you might want to add 'retired' . . . or at least, 'resting'." She stretched her arms out around her. "This sleepy backwater has been my home these past seven years. How about Pickle and I show you around? But first, you all look like you could do with food and water . . . and a 'comfort break'."

"That would be wonderful," Harper said. "The agents of the League stole all our supplies."

December extended her sword thoughtfully. "You've mentioned this League a few times now. I'm curious to know more about them."

***

"Captain Wilde," Reef said, as she led them out of the clearing. "Can we ask you a favour? We are in a spot of bother . . ."

"You think?" Captain Wilde beamed. "Stuck on a deserted island with no supplies and no seaworthy vessel!"

"Worse than that, we believe that the League may be endangering the safety of our younger students, including my sister. We would *hugely* welcome your help in staging a rescue mission. Is it possible you have a ship we might borrow?"

December Wilde laughed heartily. "I wouldn't be much of a pirate without one! Yes, I have a rather lovely old pirate junk, as it goes, moored in a sheltered cove."

Harper gasped. "*Brave as the Waves*!" she exclaimed. "She's here?!"

"That's right!" Captain Wilde said, turning to Reef. "But no, you *cannot* borrow her, boy." Seeing his gloomy expression, she nudged him in the ribs. "Don't sulk! Pickle and I will sail you wherever you want to go." Captain Wilde turned to Harper. "First rule of piracy, know your enemy! Tell me everything you know about this League of True Pirates."

As Harper and Captain Wilde strode off, deep in conversation, Antoni pulled Reef aside.

"Captain Wilde seems great," Antoni said. "Quite a character! And her ship is certainly useful. But are we absolutely sure we can trust her?"

Reef nodded. "I had the very same thought. My gut

is telling me we probably can – and, honestly, we don't have a ship-load of other options, do we?"

"True," Antoni agreed. "All the same, maybe you should send a Fishtail back to the Academy to tell the Commodore and Captain Salt they need to get out here ASAP."

Reef nodded. "You're right, of course," he said. "I'll do it just as soon as we get to shore."

He felt something bumping against his ankles and looked down to find Pickle gazing up at him, cutely. "Need a lift?" Reef enquired, crouching down and scooping the delighted boar up in his arms. The three of them hurried to catch up with Captain Wilde and Harper, who were already some distance ahead.

"Reef, I know you're worried about your sister," Antoni told his friend. "But from everything I've observed, Ocean is a pretty amazing kid."

Reef nodded, proudly. "Of course she's amazing. She's a Lermentov!"

CHAPTER 25
SWIMMING
WITH SHARKS

The three young pirates stood in a line on the shore of Spider Island, looking out to the ocean. Their small boat was tantalisingly close. But, closer still, were the circling shark fins.

"What are we going to do?" Jasmine asked.

Jacoby shook his head, fresh out of ideas. The spider bite on his hand was now throbbing like a warning siren. He had to get to their boat and get some of the anti-venom into him.

Neo began to laugh. It was the very last sound Jacoby had expected. Now, Neo began walking towards the water. Had the stress got to his brother? Should they do something before Neo willingly offered himself up as a lunchtime snack to the line of sharks?

"Neo! No!" Jacoby cried as Neo waded out into the water.

Jacoby turned to Jasmine. "I'm going in. I have to stop him."

Jasmine bit her lip. Her face mirrored Jacoby's own worry.

Now, Jacoby was in a bind. Although he had said that he was going to go into the ocean to save Neo, the very last thing he actually wanted to do was enter the shark-infested water. He walked towards the shallows, as slowly as he could manage, no longer making any effort to disguise the pain in his hand. If anything, he made it seem slightly worse.

"Come on in!" Neo called out, turning and smiling broadly. "The water's lovely!" As he spoke, a fin made its way towards his outstretched arm.

"Are you out of your mind?" Jacoby cried. "Get out of the water now! Please, Neo, you're scaring us. I don't want to lose you. I only have one *bro*—" He caught himself and quickly swallowed the rest of the word. "Neo, please just get out!"

Still, Neo didn't move. And then, when he did, he lowered himself further into the water and reached out a hand for the approaching fin. Jacoby shook his head, giving up all pretence that he was about to enter the water himself, and turned back to Jasmine.

She was watching them both curiously and walking closer to the water herself.

Neo laughed again. "Don't you see? They're whale sharks! The gentle giants of the ocean. Whale sharks pose no threats to humans. They love us, don't you, guys?"

As if on cue, the whale shark nearest Neo swam up and nuzzled him, before swimming away again to its fellows.

"Whale sharks?" Jacoby repeated, his voice hoarse. His arm was throbbing really hard now, the pain becoming worse with every passing second.

"You're absolutely sure?" Jasmine asked.

"Just look at their markings," Neo confirmed. "The Commodore was just having some fun with us."

"Well, all right, then," Jasmine said, entering the water herself. "But the fact remains that we need to get to the boat fast so we can inject Jacoby with the anti-venom."

Neo nodded, turning to Jacoby. "Are you OK to swim, buddy?"

Jacoby nodded. "Of course!" *I hope so*, he thought.

***

Back on the boat, it was action stations. The crew's first-aid kit was stored in a secure metal box with the

Barracudas' all-important emergency flares. But, as Jasmine opened the box, she frowned. "It's not in here!" she told the others, already sounding worried.

Jacoby sighed. It was hard to think clearly, especially with the throbbing bite, but he was starting to piece together what had happened. "Guys, I'm certain I did take the first-aid kit out to bring with us. I clearly remember dropping it into my kit bag."

Jasmine shook her head. "It definitely isn't in your bag now. We both went through it."

"No," Jacoby agreed, glumly. "I'm sorry," he said. "I must have dropped it somewhere along the way." A fresh thought occurred to him. "It could be somewhere on the cliff path."

Neo was instantly on his feet. "I could go back and search for it."

"You'd have to swim across to shore, then climb up that steep path and back again," Jasmine told him. "It was bad enough doing that once! And you *still* might not find it."

"I know," Neo said. "But I'm willing to give it a go."

Jacoby was dumbstruck by Neo's amazing offer. He was not only a wonderful brother but a great friend.

"Let's think," Jasmine said. "We know the other

crews are all carrying the same first-aid kits." Her face brightened. "We're coming to the end of Day Two of OB now, so we'll probably be meeting up with the other crews at the next location." She paused, turning to Jacoby. "Do you think you can hold out until then? Because I guess the other option is we set off our emergency flares right now."

"No!" Jacoby said, firmly. He knew if they let off the flares, that would bring Oceans Bound to an immediate end. He couldn't cheat everyone of this once-in-a-lifetime adventure, not for the sake of a dumb spider bite. "Definitely don't set off the flares! I'm sure I'll be fine until we meet up with the other crews."

Jasmine gazed intently at him. "Really?" she asked. "You don't need to be a hero."

Jacoby held her gaze. "Really," he told her, thinking that it might be nice to be a hero for once. "I'm fine. After everything that's been thrown at us, I want to see this adventure through."

Jasmine nodded. She shut the metal box and set it aside. "OK, I guess we sail on," she said. "In which case . . ." She reached for the blue glass bottle that had been waiting for them on their arrival back at the boat. "Neo, it's your turn to read the clue."

Neo took the bottle from her and removed the note from it.

"What does it say?" Jacoby asked, keen to distract their attention from him.

"Bravo, Barracudas!" Neo read. "You've faced snakes, spiders and sharks! Now, it's time for a relaxing sail to your next island, where," he smiled, "an important reunion awaits you."

Jasmine punched the air. "Perfect!" she said. "You see, Jacoby. We're right on course to see the other Barracudas again!"

Neo nodded, happily. "Yes! And the sooner we do that, the sooner we get hold of some anti-venom." He squeezed Jacoby's shoulder. "You're going to be all right!"

Jacoby smiled and nodded. The pain was really quite bad now but there was no need for his crewmates to know this. As soon as they found the rest of the Barracudas and got the anti-venom, he would be back to his old self. And Oceans Bound would be back on track!

CHAPTER 26
BACK TOGETHER AGAIN

Ocean expertly steered her yacht into the pretty bay. Cosmo started harrumphing that, this time, they were the *fourth* crew to arrive. Ocean didn't mind that. She scanned the figures clustered on the beach, disappointed but not surprised that Jasmine, Jacoby and Neo were not yet here.

There was a wall of noise as they arrived on the beach. Everyone was talking loudly and excitedly about the challenges they had undertaken, the close scrapes they had endured and how tired and hungry they now were.

Ocean hugged everyone hello, pleased to check in with the other crews. But, even as she hugged her friends, she found her eyes glancing back at the water, still hoping against hope to see the fifth Barracuda boat making its way into shore. When Leif came over to ask for a chat, she nodded gratefully. They walked away from the hubbub to a quiet spot on the far side of the beach.

"How are you doing?" Leif asked, sitting down on the sand and unfastening his blade leg to be more comfortable.

Ocean sat down opposite him. "Honest answer? It's like there are two of me. One Ocean is so happy to see everyone and thrilled with how we got on with our tasks today." She paused. "Then there's a second Ocean, who is deeply worried about Jasmine, Jacoby and Neo. This Ocean is pretty sure that something awful has happened to them. And she is keeping watch for them all the time." She sighed. "Am I making sense?"

Leif nodded. "I've spoken with all the other crews," he said. " No one has had any sightings of Jasmine's boat all day – not since you guys saw them slip away before breakfast."

Ocean could feel all her worst fears rushing in. "Leif, what do you think's happened?"

"I'm sorry I can't answer that," he said. "But there is one thing I am taking comfort from."

"What's that?" she asked, ready for any crumb of hope, however small.

"Jasmine's boat is equipped with the same emergency

flares as the rest of ours. If they had found themselves in major trouble out there, they would have sent up those flares."

"Yes, you're right!" Ocean was grateful for her friend's clear-headedness.

"I have given this some thought," Leif told her. "Option one is that Jasmine's crew *were* set challenges on a more remote part of the archipelago. This would account for them being late to arrive here and also for the fact we've not seen them through the day." He traced a finger in the sand before continuing. "Option two is they simply went off course at some point in the proceedings, and are having to catch up time." His eyes met Ocean's. "I think that's unlikely. Jasmine has Jacoby on navigation and he's great at that." Leif traced another shape in the sand. "Then there's option three." His eyes narrowed. "Jasmine's crew strayed from the Oceans Bound course *on purpose.*"

Ocean's head began to spin. "*On purpose?* But why would they do that?"

"There's a rumour doing the rounds with the other crews that Jasmine's Uncle Noah escaped from Federation Prison a day or two ago," Leif told her. "And that Jasmine was told this and given the choice to opt out of Oceans Bound." His eyes bore into hers. "You're her roommate and one of her best friends," he said. "Do you know anything about this?"

Feeling dazed, Ocean shook her head. "She didn't say anything to me. And we do talk about pretty much everything."

Leif shrugged, kindly. "Ocean, they *are* only rumours."

"But what if the rumours are true?"

Leif continued to make markings in the sand. Looking down, Ocean saw that he had written the letters 'LOT P'. They sent a shiver through her insides.

"If it's all true," he said, "there's a thought I can't get out of my head."

"Go on," Ocean said, feeling both fearful and intrigued.

Leif's pale-blue eyes were wide. "I think that Jasmine has been desperate – understandably – to know what has happened to her parents. I can't help but wonder if Jasmine and her crew have gone off in search of her good-for-nothing uncle."

Ocean gasped. "The three of them? On their *own*? That would be so dangerous, so reckless, so *brave* . . ." She sighed, hanging her head. "Just like Jasmine and Jacoby."

Glancing up again, she saw a figure striding across the sand towards them.

"Here you are!" Cosmo exclaimed. "I've been looking all over for you!"

"What's up?" Leif asked.

Cosmo pointed back across the beach. "So, there's a network of caves running from this side of the island to the other. According to Ari and co, who arrived here first, the Commodore's team has set up a beach party on the other side of the island. There's food, drink and games waiting for us over there! They've all gone over to make a start."

"That all sounds fun," Ocean said. She realised she didn't sound at all convincing!

"What have you two been talking about?" Cosmo asked. "No, let me guess . . . the mystery of our missing crew."

Ocean nodded. "Leif has new information and some ideas."

"Excellent!" Cosmo declared, sitting down across from them. "Let's hear what you've got."

"Don't you want to go and help the others finish setting up the party?" Ocean asked him.

Cosmo looked indignant. "How could I think about a party when my very best friend in the world –

by which I mean *you* – is so clearly hurting? And my other best friend – Jacoby Blunt – is missing at sea!" His wounded eyes met those of his friends. "Time to start talking, guys!"

**

"So," Cosmo asked Ocean, after she and Leif had shared their thinking with him. "What do you think should we do?"

Ocean only had to give it a moment's thought. "I want to go through the caves to the other side of the island and talk to the other Barracuda crews about going in search of Jasmine, Jacoby and Neo. Tonight's supper and games can wait. How can we relax and have fun when our friends might be in terrible danger?"

"Great idea!" Leif nodded, reaching for his blade and securing it back into position. "I don't think they'll take much persuading."

"Agreed," Cosmo said. "Wound one Barracuda and you wound us all. It's always been how we've done things." As he spoke, he helped Leif up to standing.

"All right then!" Ocean beamed with relief. "Let's get this rescue mission started!"

CHAPTER 27
DIGGING FOR TREASURE

"**N**ow this is more like it!" Neo declared as they sailed into a beautiful cove, fringed by circles of palm trees. The sun was starting to set and a soft golden light fell across the beach.

"Looks like we're the first to arrive," Jasmine said, bringing their boat to a stop.

Jacoby grinned. "We've been ahead of the others all day. Why stop now?"

Jasmine stared at the pretty shoreline. It looked like the perfect place to spend the evening. They were going to have so much fun here once the other Barracuda crews moored up – and they got the anti-venom sorted.

As Neo dropped anchor, she scanned the ocean for any sign of the boats. Nothing! She felt a flicker of unease but brushed it away, figuring she was just tired after everything they had been through during Day Two of Oceans Bound.

Jasmine watched Neo and Jacoby prepare the boat for its overnight mooring. They certainly made a great team. A day ago, this would have pleased her. Now, it only made her feel more like an outsider. She couldn't help but feel hurt that two of her closest friends in the world were keeping such an important secret from her.

"Sunset swim to shore!" Jacoby announced, chirpily. He seemed back to normal levels of Jacoby energy. He hadn't complained once about his bite on the sail over. Was it possible he was starting to get better already?

As if in answer to her question, Jacoby dived overboard and began swimming towards the beach. Neo waited with Jasmine as she packed up her kit bag. He was watching her carefully.

"Are you all right?" he asked.

She shrugged. "Tired. Hungry. Deeply worried about Jacoby."

He smiled kindly at her. "It's been a really long, testing day. And you've had the added pressure of being captain."

She returned his smile. "Thanks for understanding, Neo."

His eyes remained on her. "Jasmine, remember when you persuaded me to come on Oceans Bound? We promised then we'd help each other through any difficult moments." His blue-green eyes bore into hers. "I just want you to know I'm here . . . if you want to talk."

She let out a sigh, weighing up whether to say what was on her mind. She really ought to wait and give them the chance to tell her in their own time. But, before she knew it, the question was out.

"Neo, are you and Jacoby brothers?"

He flinched but held her gaze. Then he nodded. "We've been wanting so badly to tell you."

Jasmine felt instantly relieved. "I guess snakes and spiders and sharks can really get in the way of a good conversation."

"Truth." Neo laughed lightly. "How did you know?"

She shrugged. "From the first time I saw you, there was something *so* familiar about you. It took me a while to piece it together. And at the lighthouse, when you were helping Jacoby with the spiders, you called him 'brother'."

"Did I?" Neo seemed surprised. "I had no idea."

Jasmine nodded.

"Well, I'm glad you know and I'm really sorry you

had to ask," Neo said. "Hopefully, we'll get time for the three of us to talk about this, once we get Jacoby sorted."

"That would be really nice," Jasmine agreed, feeling much lighter than before.

***

Standing on the beach, Jacoby showed them the small wooden chest he had found waiting there. He opened it to reveal a scroll of paper, tied in ribbon. "Over to you, Captain!"

Jasmine lifted the scroll, slipped away the ribbon and began to read their next instructions.

"Congratulations! There's a special treat in store for the first crew to arrive here. Look up, Barracudas, then look around. X marks the spot."

Jasmine took a moment to absorb the words. Jacoby was jumping up and down, pointing to the top of the nearest palm tree. Suspended high above, in its fronds, was a spade.

"Clearly, the first part of our mission is to fetch the spade," he said. "Can I do it?"

Once more, Jasmine felt the weight of being Captain. "Are you sure you're up to it?"

Jacoby grinned. "Just watch me!"

He had always loved climbing trees and was in his

element, shinning up to the top, then windmilling his arms as if he was about to fall off, but miraculously saving himself. Jasmine found herself laughing. It really did seem as if he was back to his old self. He dropped the spade onto the sand and jumped down after it.

"Now we just need to find an X on the beach!" he declared. "Let's investigate, guys!"

As they set off together along the sand, Jasmine couldn't help but glance back to the water. Shouldn't there be *some* sign of the other crews now? The sun was setting at a rapid rate. Then she had an uplifting thought. Maybe the others had simply sailed into a cove on another side of the island. She strode after Jacoby and Neo with new energy, excited to find the treasure and then their friends.

"Here it is!" Neo cried, pointing. Just like the message laid out for them on Spider Island, an X had been made up of stones and seashells. It was situated not far from a rock face, which looked to be the entry point to a cave.

"This looks cool!" Neo said, peeling off for a moment to poke his head inside the mouth of the cave. "We should grab our lanterns and investigate later!"

"First things first!" Jacoby chivvied him. "Who's going to dig?"

"Let's take it in turns," Jasmine said. "How about I start?"

"Yes, Captain!" Jacoby said, handing over the spade.

Jasmine struck directly at the centre of the X. The first layer of sand was quite dry and, as she removed one spadeful and opened up a small hole, more sand just rushed back in to fill up the gap. At this rate, it was going to be a slow task!

Keeping going, Jasmine reached a lower layer of damper sand. At first, it made for heavy work, but it became easier to create a clear tunnel down towards their target.

"Great job, Jasmine!" Neo said, encouragingly. "Would you like me to take a turn now?"

"Actually, yes," she said, gratefully passing across the spade. She stepped back, brushing sand off her hands, to watch Neo continue the work.

***

"How much deeper do you think we need to go?" Jacoby asked.

Neo paused, sweat running down his forehead and neck. "We're getting close now. I can feel something down here." He nodded to Jacoby. "Want to take over?"

"You bet!" Jacoby seized the spade excitedly and began attacking the hole.

"Maybe a little more gently?" Neo suggested. "We don't want to break the treasure!"

"Fair point!" Jacoby said, pausing and staring down. He had unearthed what looked to be the corner of a parcel. A coloured piece of cloth was visible. "I'll finish off the job with my hands," he said. The hole was now large enough for him to stand in. Carefully, he began dislodging the treasure parcel from the clutches of the sand.

Jasmine felt her heart racing as she saw the package revealed. She instantly recognised that the coloured cloth belonged to a Pirate Federation flag. Jacoby passed the parcel to her carefully. She took it from him and sat down, brushing the last stray grains of sand from the cloth flag. Jacoby and Neo came over to sit on either side of her.

Jasmine started to unwrap the parcel. The large flag had been folded and wrapped in many layers. She could feel her anticipation building as she turned the package in her hands, watched closely by her friends.

She saw a burst of white and then a flash of gold, but she didn't realise at first what it was. Then, as she rolled the flag one more time, a skull fell out of the folds of material.

Neo and Jacoby both gasped. A stunned Jasmine cradled the skull in her hands. The bone felt cool to the touch. She stared at the empty eye sockets, her heart thumping wildly.

"Who is this?" she asked aloud, frowning. "Who *was* this?"

"Something else fell out when you made the final turn," Neo told her. He reached across the sand and scooped up a pool of gold chain. "It's a locket," he said, holding it up into the light of the setting sun. As the locket turned, the familiar emblem of a peacock was revealed. Jasmine felt her blood turn to ice. Then she felt violently sick.

"Jasmine?" Neo asked. "Are you OK?"

She shook her head. She was going to *be* sick. She jumped urgently to her feet and raced off towards the mouth of the cave. As she ran, the skull slipped from her fingers, down onto the sand.

"Let me see that," Jacoby told Neo, reaching for the locket. As he took it and inspected it, he frowned. "This is Jasmine's father's locket," he informed Neo. "Captain Jonathan Peacock always wore it. See the peacock crest? Inside will be pictures of Jasmine and her mother."

Neo nodded, his eyes wide with horror. "If that's

Jasmine's dad's locket, does that mean that the skull ..."
He left the horrible question hanging in the warm air.

Jacoby rose to his feet. He looked furious now, his face stained red by the setting sun. "I don't think we're playing by the Commodore's rules anymore," he said. "Someone else has taken control of the game."

Jasmine heard her friends' words and saw them look towards each other, fearfully. But, as she started to walk back to them, she found she couldn't move. Someone had her in a stranglehold. She opened her mouth to cry out but a gloved hand instantly covered her mouth to silence her cry. Then she was pulled backwards into the mouth of the cave.

CHAPTER 28
THE CAVE

For a time, nothing made much sense. It was dark, but there were whirling pools of light. She was moving at speed, but not of her own free will, her feet skimming the uneven ground beneath her. She was held in the clutches of someone much taller and stronger. The air was, by turns, dry then damp. Then she felt a sharp breeze. At last, everything began to settle.

Jasmine found herself standing on smooth stone, still tightly held in the grip of adult hands. Facing her was a figure, visible only by the light of a lantern. Her eyes traced the outline of dark clothes, a cloak and, glinting in the lantern light, the horribly familiar mask of a pretty ship's figurehead. Wide, staring eyes, the thinnest of eyebrows, flushed cheeks and a pouting rosebud of a mouth. Then the mask lifted and Jasmine found herself gazing into the even more familiar face of a suntanned and unshaven Uncle Noah.

"Hello, Jasmine," he said. "It's wonderful to see my favourite niece again." Slipping the mask fully over his head of unruly red-gold curls, he smiled more broadly. "I had a feeling fate would bring us together."

This made her angry. "I don't think you can call it fate, Uncle Noah, when you track me over the oceans, then drag me by force into a dank cave."

"Sometimes, we have to give fate a little nudge." His bright eyes met hers. "Just to be clear, dear niece, it wasn't your Uncle No who did the dragging." He nodded above her head. "I believe you have met my comrade, Captain Cecile Binoche."

The name was instantly familiar to her. Now, as Jasmine was released and Captain Binoche lifted her own mask, she knew why. Cecile Binoche had been one of two LOT P agents who had threatened Neo at the Academy Harbour. Soon after, she had been taken into Federation custody.

Jasmine turned back to her uncle. "I hear you escaped from the Pirate Federation's maximum-security prison," she said.

He nodded. "Turns out it's more 'minimum security' – wouldn't you agree, Captain Binoche?"

His companion laughed. The sound echoed in the

cave in an eerie way.

"Well, Jasmine," Uncle Noah said now. "You don't seem overjoyed to see me."

Jasmine's heart was racing. She was frightened – how could she not be? – but also angry. She hoped her fear might not be obvious in the meagre light provided by Noah's lantern. She folded her arms and stared up at him, crossly.

"I have a feeling you've been the puppet-master behind our adventures today," she said. "The snakes, the spiders, the sharks . . ." She broke off. "And the skull. None of these were part of the real Oceans Bound, were they?"

Uncle Noah looked impressed. "Very good, Jasmine. You're right that the route your crew has taken today was something of a detour from the Commodore's OG plans." He shrugged. "Sorry for all this . . . cloak and dagger stuff. It's just how the higher powers in the League like to do things."

"The higher powers?" Jasmine said. "When we last met, you told me there were no ranks, other than ability, in the League."

Uncle Noah smiled. "I'm flattered you remember our conversation, word-for-word."

Captain Binoche cleared her throat. "We should be on our way, Captain Ripley, if we're going to make our next *rendez-vous*."

"Just a minute!" Uncle Noah's eyes returned to Jasmine. "I wonder then, have you thought any more about joining us?" His eyes glinted in the lantern-light. "I really do think this could be the making of you."

She shook her head. "I am not interested in joining the League, Uncle. And I never will be."

He shrugged, calmly. "Never say never, dear niece."

"We really do have to go," Captain Binoche cut in, pushing Jasmine forwards quite roughly.

"Where are you taking me?" Jasmine asked. "I assume I am your prisoner now?"

Uncle Noah shook his head. "No, Jasmine. You are *not* our prisoner. We have made some advance travel plans and you are most welcome to join us. But you would be coming of your own free will – as our guest."

Jasmine's eyes narrowed. "I really don't understand."

"You read the last note," Uncle Noah said. "We promised you a reunion."

"I thought that note meant getting back together with the Barracudas," Jasmine said. "How dumb was that?"

Noah smiled. "Not dumb at all."

Now Jasmine frowned. "And then, when we unearthed the skull, and my dad's locket, I thought you meant the reunion was with—" She broke off, feeling a strong wave of emotion rising inside her. "Uncle Noah, how could *you* do that to *me*?"

"There, there," he said, reaching out a hand to stroke her hair. "You didn't actually think the skull belonged to your father, did you?"

"No," Jasmine said through tight lips. "I didn't think that. I mean, it's not impossible that a human skull would decompose so quickly, but the odds are very much against it."

"You see!" Noah announced, proudly. "It's that kind of grace and calm under extreme pressure. That's why you'd be such a terrific asset."

"Over my dead body!" Jasmine told him, defiantly.

"No need for hasty decision-making," Uncle Noah said. "We'll have time to discuss this later as a *family*." He crouched down before Jasmine, holding the lantern up above his head so both their faces were lit in the same warm pool of light. "I promised you a reunion and your *Uncle No* always keeps his word. Now, if you come with us, I can promise you the *mother* of all reunions."

"Mother!" This time, Jasmine's own high-pitched

voice was the echo.

Uncle Noah nodded, smiling.

Jasmine's heart was racing again. After everything this day had thrown at her, could her uncle's words be true? He was speaking in riddles – nothing new there. But if there was even a chance he was going to take her to her mother, she was willing to follow.

"Yes," she told him, feeling a wave of tiredness but also fresh courage. "I'll come with you."

CHAPTER 29
BETWEEN A ROCK AND A HARD PLACE

"Where *is* she?" Jacoby asked Neo for the third time.

Neo shook his head. He could hear the rising panic each time Jacoby spoke. They both needed to keep calm. Which wasn't easy when your friend and crewmate had disappeared into thin air. Especially when this happened moments after digging up a skull. Neo shuddered.

There was no way this 'dig up your dad's skull' task was part of the Oceans Bound challenge course. Jacoby had nailed it when he said that someone else had taken control. Neo now watched as Jacoby draped Jasmine's dad's locket around his own neck.

"For safekeeping," Jacoby said.

Neo nodded, deep in thought. The burial of the skull with Jonathan Peacock's locket bore all the signs of LOT P. They loved their riddles and their cruel tricks.

It seemed highly likely that Neo and his friends could thank LOT P for the snakes, spiders and sharks as well as the skull. The thought set off a chain-reaction in his belly – a sharp twist of fear. Because, if this was all true, then the agents of the League were likely very close now. He and Jacoby had to find Jasmine before LOT P got to her.

"She must have gone into the cave!" Jacoby exclaimed. "It's the only explanation."

"The cave?" Neo turned towards the gaping entry. "Why on oceans would she do that?"

Jacoby shrugged, helplessly. "I don't know. But, unless you have any better ideas, I'm going in after her." He strode towards the entrance. Was it Neo's imagination or was Jacoby walking a little unevenly? Could this be the impact of spider venom seeping deeper into his body? They urgently needed the anti-venom. Which meant finding the other crews. Which, most likely, meant sailing away from this island. And abandoning Jasmine to her fate.

Noooo! Don't make me choose between them!

Neo felt a searing pain in his head.

"Jacoby!" he called. "I'll go in. You wait here. You need to rest up. I'll go search for Jasmine and then we'll find the other crews and get you the anti-venom."

Jacoby looked back at Neo, calmly shaking his head. "If you think I'm going to sit around on the sand while Jasmine faces who knows what kind of danger, you don't know me at all."

"OK, but wait!" Neo glanced out to where their yacht was moored. The crew's emergency flares were kept on the boat. Maybe it was time to set them off and bring Oceans Bound to an immediate end? But swimming to the boat would take precious time.

Neo glanced back towards Jacoby, just in time to see his brother disappear into the cave. OK, that decided it. He couldn't let Jacoby go any further on his own.

He raced across the sand to retrieve his kit bag, and let out a sigh of relief. In addition to the emergency flares, each Barracuda had also been given a personal supply of smaller flares which you could hold in your hand and would provide a few minutes of light at a time. Without wasting a second more, Neo raced back to the cave.

He struck the first flare on the rock at the entrance. Immediately, it bloomed into a bright red light. That should give them their first four minutes. Maybe, if they were lucky, that would be enough.

"Jasmine!" Jacoby called out. "Jasmine, are you in here?"

They both drew still, hearing the echo of Jacoby's cry, waiting for a response. There wasn't one. Neo moved into lead position. The ground beneath them was uneven. He pointed to Jacoby to watch his step. Despite his bite, Jacoby seemed as energetic as always – actually, even more so. Neo suspected Jacoby's body was flooded with adrenaline. This worried him. What if, like the flare in Neo's hand, Jacoby's energy could only last so long?

Tamping down this fear, Neo forged onwards, his eyes scanning the edges of the cave for some sign of Jasmine. The deeper they journeyed into the cave, the more Neo realised just how vast it was. Turning, he waited for Jacoby to catch up. "You good to go?" Neo asked.

Jacoby grimaced but nodded. Neo struck the second flare on the cave wall. As they hastened onwards, they came to a fork, with two tunnels spiralling off in different directions.

"Should we split up?" Jacoby asked.

"No," Neo said, firmly. "We stay together. And you need to keep sipping water."

"OK," Jacoby said, obediently reaching for his flask. "Pick a tunnel then!"

"The right-hand one," Neo said.

Jacoby followed, keeping pace. As the tunnel wormed its way through the cave, it became more and more narrow, until they had to move in single file. The roof had lowered too and, as Neo continued on, he could feel his hair brushing the uneven rock of the ceiling.

Neo called out Jasmine's name but still she didn't answer. He turned to check on Jacoby and found his brother was no longer at his side but a little way behind. Neo had been right. Jacoby's energy *was* beginning to drain away. Now, as if in sympathy, the second flare dwindled. Heart racing, Neo reached into his pack for the next.

"Wait!" Jacoby told him. "Before you waste another flare, there's something I need to say to you." Neo froze. In the last light from the dying flare, he could see the pain painted across his brother's face. "Neo, this is *really* important."

CHAPTER 30
JACOBY'S LAST WORDS

Neo wanted desperately to keep on moving but he also recognised the urgency in Jacoby's voice. He waited for his brother to speak.

"You might need to go on without me," Jacoby told him, calmly. "The pain is getting worse. Quite a lot worse. Neo, I'm not sure I'm going to make it."

"Nonsense!" Neo cried. "We just need to get you the anti-venom." He made a snap decision. "We're going back the way we came," he said. "We're going back to the beach and the boat and I'm raising the full emergency flares."

"No, listen!" Jacoby's voice was strong again. "You have to keep on, Neo. You have to find Jasmine and bring her back safe. And when you do, tell her how sorry I am."

"You can tell her yourself when you see her," Neo said, carefully.

"Maybe," Jacoby replied. "But just in case I can't."

"We should walk and talk," Neo said, lifting the flare to strike it against the low ceiling.

"No!" Jacoby said. "Don't waste it!"

Too late. Neo held the lit flare in his hand. Now he could see that Jacoby was in a crumpled heap, scrunched against the cave wall. He looked pale – as if the light had gone out inside him. Now Neo was really worried.

"You have to get up!" Neo told him. "We need to get you out of here, back to—"

"Wait!" Jacoby raised his bite-free hand. "This won't take long. I just need you to tell her . . . it was all about my fear. From the day I was born, I thought I was marked out to be extraordinary. I saw my brilliant future. *Commodore Jacoby Rawdon Blunt.* My parents, my sisters, drummed it into me that I was going to be a pirate superstar. Then I arrived at Pirate Academy and the teachers started telling me the same thing . . . I totally believed the hype."

Neo frowned. They really did need to get moving again. But he could feel the importance of what Jacoby wanted to say.

"Then I had that terrible report, the very night you arrived at the Academy. That report pulled me up sharp. I was so determined to be chosen as a Captain for Oceans Bound. Because I told myself that if I got chosen, that means I still have a chance . . . that Jacoby Blunt could still be extraordinary." He broke off, tears washing down his pale face. "But now I know. I'm just average. Middle of the ocean. Probably talented enough to be a reliable Deputy. But not marked out for any kind of glory." He shook his head. "I was frightened to face it before, but now I've made my peace with it. I'm not going to be one of the extraordinary ones, Neo. And that's OK. When you next see Jasmine, please tell her."

Neo crouched down in front of his brother. It was crazy to think how much this crumpled human had come to mean to him in the short time they had known each other. His eyes met Jacoby's. The very same blue-green eyes as Neo's own.

"Listen to me," Neo said. "You're not thinking clearly right now, because you're tired and weak from that evil bite. But the truth is, Jacoby Blunt, you *are* extraordinary. You might not see it, but I do. Jasmine does too."

Tears streamed down Jacoby's face. "I just wish we'd had the chance to tell her that we're brothers," he said.

The third flare went out. "She already knows," Neo said. "She figured it out herself."

"She did?" Jacoby's voice was soft. "Was she OK with us keeping it secret?"

"Yes," Neo told him.

"That's good," Jacoby said, sounding as if he was about to drop off to sleep. "That's—"

"Enough talk!" Neo said. "We're heading back to the boat right now."

When Jacoby didn't answer, Neo reached out to squeeze his brother's shoulder. As he did so, he realised Jacoby's head was slumped forwards onto his chest. His body was as limp as a ragdoll. If they were ever going to get out of this cave, Neo was going to have to carry him.

CHAPTER 31
RESCUE MISSION

cean felt like she was walking on air. Leif had been right. It had taken seconds for all the remaining Barracudas to agree to the rescue mission. And minutes for them to halt their supper preparations. Now, as they made their way back through the cave network – towards the other side of the island and their boats – the Barracudas' spirits were high and their voices noisy.

"This is *exactly* what Oceans Bound is all about," said Ari, striding alongside Ocean. "Not the part about our friends being in danger, obviously," she clarified. "But about us, away from our teachers, making the right judgement calls." She smiled at Ocean. "Seems you're a natural born leader, Ocean Lermentov. But I guess we already knew that."

There was some discussion, bordering on disagreement, about how best to cross through the cave network to the beach on the north side of the island, where they had earlier moored their boats. It seemed that some of the Barracudas had taken one route through the caves whilst others – including Ocean, Cosmo and Leif – had traversed it in an entirely different way. Both routes had brought them out at the desired location but there was much debate as to which was faster. Now that the decision had been taken to get back to the boats, and set sail on the rescue mission, no one wanted to waste a single second.

"Ocean should decide!" Leif's voice cut through the hubbub. "Don't you think?"

"Yes!" Ari agreed. "One hundred per cent. This is Ocean's call."

Ocean pointed to the left. "I vote we take this tunnel," she said. "From what I remember, it is single file but it's pretty direct." Once again, nobody objected.

***

They were some distance into the tunnel when Ocean, still leading the others, noticed movement ahead of her. She paused and lifted her lantern to see better but the figure was too far away.

"What's up?" asked Cosmo, who was close behind and now walked right into her.

"I saw someone up ahead," Ocean told him.

"Friend or foe?" Cosmo enquired, playfully.

"Let's see!" Ocean continued on her way, walking faster now, taking advantage of the fact that the narrow tunnel was at last beginning to open out. She found Cosmo striding along at her side as they turned a corner and she saw the figure again.

"There!" she pointed. Then her heart missed a beat. "Neo!" she cried. "Neo, is that you?"

Neo paused to turn. He seemed to be carrying something heavy. The light from their lanterns might be dim but the exhausted expression on Neo's face was all too clear to read.

"Neo!" Ocean cried again, running towards him. "What's wrong? Where are—"

Her voice fell away as she saw that the thing Neo was carrying was Jacoby. Drawing her lantern closer, Ocean saw that Jacoby's eyelids were closed and his face was as pale as bone.

"Whatever has happened to him?" It was Cosmo who asked the question, surging ahead and inspecting his friend, with a worried frown.

"He's taken a bad spider bite," Neo told them, his voice low and tired. "He desperately needs anti-venom but we've lost our supply. Can we borrow some?"

"Don't worry!" Cosmo said. "We're on our way to our boats."

Neo looked close to tears with relief. "Thank you," he rasped. "You got here just in time."

"Time to give you a break!" Cosmo turned to call over his shoulder. "Leif, can you come over and help me carry Jacoby?" Leif immediately ran forwards.

As Cosmo and Leif took Jacoby carefully from Neo's arms, Ocean fell into step with Neo.

"Neo," she said, "it's wonderful to see you and Jacoby again. But where is Jasmine?"

In answer, Neo's face fell and he shook his head, sadly. Ocean felt waves of fresh fear pulsing through her veins. What had happened to her friend and roomie?

CHAPTER 32
DEPARTURES AND ARRIVALS

Jasmine followed Uncle Noah silently on through the cave, thoughts racing in her head. She was desperate to see her mum again, but could she fully trust Noah's word that he would indeed bring the two of them together?

No! She answered herself. She couldn't trust Noah Ripley any further than she could throw him. But, strangely, a strong feeling in her gut told her to believe him this time.

Jasmine felt bad about leaving Jacoby and Neo just when Jacoby's spider bite was obviously getting much worse. He had looked really pale and poorly when she'd last seen him on the beach. But, she told herself, Jacoby was in the best hands – his brother's hands. Neo had proved to be calm and dependable in a crisis. She knew that he would do everything in his power to get Jacoby the anti-venom, even if that meant setting off the flares that would summon the Academy captains and bring Oceans Bound to an abrupt end.

Her thoughts were interrupted as she glimpsed daylight piercing the darkness ahead. They must be close now to exiting the cave. Jasmine felt her heart lift. She wondered how her mum was feeling about seeing her again. Then she frowned, reminding herself that her mother was a prisoner of the League. Uncle Noah probably hadn't even told her yet.

"Wait!" she called out, the word slipping from her mouth before she could catch it. "Before I come with you, I want to get some things clear."

"Tick, tock," Captain Binoche tutted behind her. "Tick, tock."

"It's okay, Jasmine," Noah said. "What's on your mind?"

She took a breath. "Taking us off course, throwing all those horrible challenges at us . . ." Her eyes were wet as they met her uncle's. "What was this all about? Were you trying to break me before persuading me to come with you? Or to test me out, see what I was made of?"

Uncle Noah considered her words, then smiled softly at her. "Maybe that was part of it. But what you need to understand is that, as important as you are to me personally, this goes far beyond you." He folded his arms across his chest. "The League of True Pirates has a message that the Pirate Federation needs to hear loud and clear."

"A message?" Jasmine echoed.

Uncle Noah nodded. "It's a simple one. No Federation location is safe. The time when they ruled the oceans is at an end." He shrugged. "Maybe your Commodore and his cronies will understand that now. And now, we really do need to get going."

Jasmine followed him out into the light. She felt numb. Since they had entered the cave, the sun had begun to set. Now they were back outside again, the island was bathed in warm orange, pink and purple light.

They had come out onto a rocky outcrop, higher above the ocean waters than on the island's other side. Uncle Noah led the way over the rock. Jasmine saw there was a boat waiting for them down in the lapping waters. The small boat, just a little bigger than one of the Academy yachts, was

painted black and flew the LOT P flag. Inside, another masked agent of the League was waiting for them.

Jasmine allowed Noah to help her onto the boat. Captain Binoche jumped across to join them.

"Next stop, the shipyard!" Uncle Noah announced, taking the wheel.

"Yes, Captain Ripley," said the one remaining masked agent.

There was immediately something familiar about that voice. The agent lifted the mask and let it rest on the back of her head. She now smiled openly at Jasmine.

"Jasmine, it's nice to see you again!" said Priya Swift, Jasmine's former classmate.

***

"I don't understand, Neo." Ocean's ice-blue eyes showed both anger and hurt. "How can you *not* know where Jasmine is? We thought you guys had gone off-grid in order to search for Jasmine's Uncle Noah."

"No!" Neo rasped. "No, that's not it at all." As they strode side-by-side through the cave, he tried his best to explain. He started with the snakes, spiders and sharks, because those all felt important now. Then, how they had dug up the skull – which may or may not have been Jonathan Peacock, Jasmine's dad –

along with the captain's locket. How Jasmine had felt sick and run off towards the cave. And then, a split second later, disappeared.

Ocean's eyes were wide throughout Neo's explanation. She listened carefully and didn't interrupt once. When he finished speaking, she shook her head and reached her hand to his arm. "Neo, I'm so sorry. I think LOT P has been playing cruel games with your crew."

He nodded. "I think so too." He looked ahead to where Cosmo and Leif were dragging a lifeless Jacoby, his sailing shoes skimming the floor of the cave. "Do you think this is what they wanted?" Neo asked Ocean. "One of us missing, another taking a maybe fatal spider bite? Do they just want to create pain and chaos, or do they have a plan?"

"I think they use chaos as a cloak to disguise their evil plans," Ocean told him. "The one thing I think we can safely assume is that they have now taken Jasmine."

Neo shuddered. "I'm really worried for Jasmine," he said. "But, Ocean, we *have* to get Jacoby the anti-venom. I don't know how long—"

"Yes," Ocean nodded. "Jacoby's our first priority. Then we go in search of Jasmine. Once we get back to our boats, we can set off the emergency flares to signal to the Commodore." She flashed him a smile. "You're a total hero, Neo. It must have been awful for you feeling like you had to choose which of your friends to save. Just know you're not on your own now."

Neo smiled gratefully. "Thanks, Ocean. I know how much Jasmine means to you."

"She and I might as well be sisters," Ocean agreed. "I'm so grateful to you for doing everything in your power to look out for her."

Neo felt a fresh surge of hope. As they marched onwards, he suddenly saw light at the end of the tunnel – and sand and palm trees beyond. Ocean quickly explained that their target was the beach on the north side of the island, where the four Barracuda boats were moored. Neo realised his own crew must have moored their boat on the island's east side.

But, as he and Ocean emerged from the cave and set foot on the sand, all Neo's new-found hope and relief instantly drained away at the chaotic scene in front of him.

"Noooooooooo!" Ocean cried, racing ahead over the sand. "This cannot be happening!"

Neo caught her up, trying to make sense of it all as he ran. The four Barracuda boats that had been moored here were still in the water, but they had been joined by three larger LOT P vessels. Masked LOT P agents had crossed from their own boats onto the Academy yachts and hoisted anchor. Already three of the Barracuda crew's boats had been captured and masked LOT P agents were now targeting the last remaining boat, moored closest to shore.

"That's *my* boat!" Ocean cried out. "And there's no way *they* are taking it!" Her face showed icy determination. "Our medical supplies are on board. And our emergency flares too! We have to stop them!" She reached into her kit bag, drew out her dagger and let the bag fall to the sand. Her ice-blue eyes were suddenly full of fire. "This fight just got real."

CHAPTER 33
CLOSE COMBAT

Everything happened at breakneck pace. At Ocean's urging, Neo and Cosmo stayed on the sand with Jacoby. "Keep talking to him!" she cried over her shoulder, as she raced towards the water, flanked by Shay and Leif. "He needs to hear *your* voices."

Ocean, Shay and Leif raced on into the water, to lead the fight to take back Ocean's boat. For most people, swimming with an outstretched dagger would have proved cumbersome. But most people did not have the benefit of five years of elite Pirate Academy training. The Barracudas cleverly deployed their weapons to swim even faster out to the target boat.

As the remaining eight Barracudas emerged from the cave, they swiftly took stock of the emergency situation and, without delay, raced down to the water's edge to join the fray. Neo swelled with pride as he watched his classmates come together as a crew. He thought of

Ocean's earlier words. *Just know you're not on your own now. We're all here.*

In the water, two LOT P agents had made it onto Ocean's boat and were now attempting to haul anchor. Before they could do so, Ocean, Shay and Leif had reached the yacht and were trying to climb on board.

One of the agents tried to hold them off while the other one continued to work on the anchor. Moving in perfect formation, Shay and Leif succeeded in wrong-footing the first agent and sent them splashing down, head-first, into the water. As they fell, their sword slipped from their hand and bounced into the hull.

The agent quickly surfaced, mask askew, and attempted to climb back onto the boat to retrieve the sword. The double act of Shay and Leif showed them no mercy, forcing them back down into the water. The agent continued to struggle for a time but, as the two Barracudas directed their daggers straight at the enemy's neck, it was crystal clear who was in control now. Shay and Leif held the LOT P agent hostage as eight of their energetic classmates swam out to offer further support.

Meanwhile, Ocean had climbed back onto her boat to face down the remaining LOT P agent. Ocean Lermentov was known to be incredibly agile. The agent who had boarded her boat was forced to abandon the mission to hoist anchor. They now drew a sword and extended it towards Ocean. Neo watched, heart in his mouth, as Ocean and the LOT P agent were drawn into close combat.

The agent was bigger and taller than Ocean but the young Barracuda had the twin advantage of her elite Academy training and her unrivalled natural athleticism. Plus, as Ocean moved forwards, she had scooped up the enemy sword that had fallen into the hull. Dagger in her left hand, sword in her right, she prepared to fight for her vessel.

Across the water, Neo heard Ocean's sword clashing against her enemy's. He knew his classmate would be pouring every drop of her anger against LOT P – and her worry for Jasmine and Jacoby – into this fight. He hoped it would be enough for her to seize victory.

"Look!" Cosmo shouted, suddenly. "The other crews are on the move!"

Neo was reluctant to tear his eyes away from Ocean for even a second, but he allowed himself the briefest glance. He figured the other agents would be coming to rescue their comrades but, to his surprise, the remaining LOT P vessels – along with the stolen Barracuda boats –

had begun sailing away in a flotilla. Neo's heart pumped furiously. Had the other agents concluded it was only a matter of time before their comrade overpowered Ocean? Or had they simply decided to cut their losses and stick to their fiendish plan?

Returning his attention to the deck of Ocean's boat, he was just in time to see the LOT P agent take a sword swipe at Ocean. At last, Ocean was wrong-footed. Neo held his breath as the agent surged forwards to drive home the advantage. Neo couldn't bear the thought that, after all her prowess and bravery, Ocean was about to be defeated.

He needn't have worried. What the agent hadn't seen was that the other Barracudas had now reached the vessel. Most remained in the water, helping Shay and Leif to fully overpower the first agent. But two of the Barracudas nimbly climbed up from the stern of the Academy yacht. As the agent took what they supposed to be the fatal swipe at Ocean, they were blind to the approach of Ari and Rose from behind them.

Ocean jumped off the boat and the agent reared up in a horrid victory dance. But, as they turned back towards the anchor, they found themselves now facing a deadly pincer movement from two of the Academy's finest young sword-hands. The agent was taken totally by surprise. As they wrestled to contain the dual threat, they were unaware of Ocean climbing back onto the bow of her boat. Now the enemy was fully surrounded.

Ocean let out a warrior cry as she took a flying lunge at the agent. She knocked the sword out of their hand and it splashed down into the water. Now the agent had no weapon to fight the three Barracudas, who were each equipped with a deadly blade and the expertise in how to use it. Neo could imagine the smiles on the faces of Ari, Rose and Ocean as they closed in on the broken enemy who, at last, raised their hands to signal defeat.

There were cheers from the other Barracudas in the water and, on the beach, from Neo and Cosmo too.

"Did you see that, old friend?" Cosmo asked Jacoby. "That was quite some fight – and all on your behalf!"

Jacoby did not answer. But Neo thought perhaps his eyelids did flicker to show some kind of recognition.

"It was incredible!" Neo said, flooding all his remaining energy into his own voice, in the hope it might help reach Jacoby.

Neo's heart lifted. He was pretty sure that Jacoby was smiling.

Meanwhile, over on the one remaining Academy

yacht, Ocean, Ari and Rose set off the emergency flares. Neo watched them soar into the sky like fireworks. Oceans Bound was now officially at an end and help would soon be on the way.

Neo felt a strange mix of emotions. He was flooded with relief – and hope that they would now get Jasmine back safely. But, all the same, he couldn't help but wonder if the Barracudas might have saved the day without back-up, all on their own.

CHAPTER 34
BROTHERS

Four figures sat in a line on the sand.

"Would you like to do the honours, Neo?" Ocean enquired, now that the large, sharp needle loaded with high-dosage anti-venom was ready to apply.

Neo grimaced. "I'm not great with needles," he admitted.

"Here, let me!" Cosmo said, grabbing the needle out of Ocean's hands and pushing it down into Jacoby's exposed chest. "Been wanting to stab this one ever since Clam Class!"

The impact of the anti-venom was amazingly fast. First Jacoby's eyes popped open, as if he had just woken from the deepest, most restful sleep. Then his entire upper body bolted upright, like he'd been given an electric shock. This transformation was a huge relief but a bit unsettling at the same time.

"Take it easy, old pal!" Cosmo warned him, as Neo

and Ocean rushed to support him, in case he slumped backwards and did himself an injury. But Jacoby showed no sign of slumping. He seemed instantly possessed of vital new energy.

"My name is Jacoby Rawdon Blunt," he declared, as if introducing himself in a quiz tournament. "I am eleven years old and I'm in Barracuda Class at Pirate Academy, Coral Sea Province—"

"Yes, you are!" Cosmo was grinning from ear to ear. But Jacoby hadn't quite finished.

"My parents are Beaufort and Clothilde Blunt, Captain and Deputy of *The North Star*. I have three sisters – Izzy, Roxy and Savannah – and—"

Realising what was likely coming next, Neo tried to think of something, *anything*, to say to drown out Jacoby but he found himself too stunned and too tired as, sure enough, Jacoby forged on: "—and one awesome brother!"

Cosmo looked askance at Jacoby. "You have a *brother*?" He chuckled heartily.

Jacoby smiled, reaching his hand across to clasp Neo's. "I have an awesome brother and his name is Neo. And the best part is he's not only my brother but one of my best friends."

Neo's heart was racing. He was aware of Ocean now

looking at him suspiciously. But Cosmo roared with laughter. "Oh Jacoby, the anti-venom is making you say the strangest things!" Cosmo grinned at Neo. "Can you imagine anything worse than being Jacoby's brother?!"

Neo forced himself to smile and roll his eyes. "Very funny," he said. "But now we have Jacoby back on track, we really need to think about going off in search of Jasmine."

"Ocean set off our emergency flares," Cosmo pointed out. "I know you're worried about Jasmine – we all are. But I think we can wait for reinforcements to arrive now. I'm sure they won't take—"

"They're already here!" Ocean said, up on her feet and pointing out to sea, where a new ship was cresting the waves towards them. Neo watched Ocean's expression shift. "Unless that's LOT P returning to take back our prisoners?"

Neo's eyes travelled across the beach from the tall palm tree to which they had expertly tied the two captured LOT P agents, then back out to the water and the ship Ocean was talking about. It didn't, at first glance, look like a LOT P ship. It was considerably bigger than the vessels LOT P had sailed to the island on. This was an elegant full-sized pirate junk.

Neo pointed. "It's flying the Pirate Federation flag!" he said. "I think we're safe."

"If my brother says we're safe," Jacoby contributed, "we are definitely safe!"

Ignoring Jacoby, Cosmo stalked over to join Neo and Ocean. "Couldn't be some kind of trick, could it?" The three of them held their breath.

The ship had moored in the deeper waters of the bay but now a small tender appeared from around the side of it. The boat was being rowed towards the beach. As it came nearer, four figures became visible on board. At the front was a striking woman with a cloud of colourful hair, a mouth full of gemstones and a small pig in her arms. Neo let out a sigh and smiled. It had been a while but there could be no mistaking December Wilde.

Neo glanced at Ocean, whose eyes remained fixed on the tender. He watched her suddenly start jumping up and down on the sand, waving her arms in the air. Turning back to Neo and Cosmo, she beamed. "It's Reef, my brother! And his mates Harper and Antoni from Stingray Class," she explained. "They've been setting the Oceans Bound course for us. Don't know who the woman is with them, but she looks like quite a character!" Turning back to the water, Ocean roared. "Reef Lermentov! What took you so long?!"

CHAPTER 35
BREAKING THE RULES

The Barracudas raced across the sand to welcome the new arrivals. Neo and Cosmo helped Jacoby to his feet but he insisted he could walk on unaided.

"Ocean!" cried a tall, blonde boy, as he stepped from the water to the sand. As Ocean rushed over to greet her brother, the family likeness was obvious.

"Ocean, I've been *so* worried about you!" Reef told her, patting her on the back.

Leif stepped forwards. "It's natural for a brother to worry about his kid sister but, you should know, Ocean has been our wonderfully brave leader today."

"Really?" Reef smiled at the nods and shouts of agreement from the crowd in front of him.

"Where have you been?" Ocean asked. "You were setting the course for us, right?"

Reef nodded. "Long story, short. Yes – Harper, Antoni and I were in charge of your course. But, last night, we ran into Noah Ripley and some of his LOT P comrades. They left us tied up on what we thought was a deserted island—"

"Only it wasn't deserted, see?" boomed a voice from behind him. "It was *my* island. My name, for those of you who don't know me yet, is December Wilde." She stepped forwards and instantly captured everyone's attention. Neo smiled. With her extravagant hair and her bejewelled mouth, December Wilde had always had the air of a rock superstar. "I'm a pirate captain," she continued. "Lately I've been living the quiet life in this lazy backwater." She stroked her pig tenderly, then set him down on the sand to have a run. "Only, turns out, this backwater's not quite so lazy as it used to be."

"Not since Noah Ripley and his pals appeared," Reef added.

"LOT P were here too," Ocean told him.

"Some of them still *are*," Ari said, pointing towards their two prisoners.

"We believe Noah Ripley has captured his niece Jasmine," Ocean said, urgently. She put her arms around Jacoby and Neo. "These poor guys have had everything thrown at them today – from spider-bites to skulls!"

"Then LOT P came here and captured most of our boats," Ari said. "We succeeded in saving Ocean's boat but they sailed off with the other three."

"They've probably taken Jasmine's boat also," Leif cut in. "It was moored on the East coast of the island."

"You say they've taken Jasmine Peacock?" December Wilde asked now.

"We think so," Ocean nodded, urgently. "Only we don't know where."

"They departed in a north-north-east direction," Leif added.

"That's helpful," Captain Wilde said. "If they're sailing north-north-east from here, chances are they're heading for Atafutura Atoll. There have been some whispers on the water recently of fresh activity over there."

"Captain Wilde," Ocean said, taking charge again. "Will you take us there?"

Captain Wilde nodded. "With pleasure . . . Ocean, is it? Cool name! We can rope your yacht to my junk."

"Captain Wilde," Reef interrupted. "I thought we agreed we would wait for the Commodore and Captain Salt to arrive to discuss our next move."

Captain Wilde dropped to her knees, scooping up her pet pig. "I haven't known you long," she said, "but I have come to realise, Reef Lermentov, that you do like to follow rules."

Reef ran a hand nervously through his long blonde hair. "Is that such a bad thing?"

Captain Wilde drew herself up to her full height. "It's not *necessarily* a bad thing. But following rules isn't the only way to get things done."

As Reef fumbled to respond, his younger sister jumped in. "Just suppose, Captain Wilde, we decided to *break* the rules? Suppose we decided to seize the amazing good fortune of you arriving here, with a ship big enough to carry us all, and we followed the LOT P boats to Atafutura Atoll to rescue Jasmine and find out what exactly is going on there?"

Captain Wilde beamed, displaying her dazzling bejewelled mouth. "I, for one, would find that a far more interesting way to proceed." She became suddenly serious. "Also, if this Ripley character *has* captured his niece – then we don't want to waste time here, do we?"

"I agree," Ocean nodded. There were cries of support from the other Barracudas.

Reef shook his head. "But I already sent a Fishtail to brief the Commodore. And you guys set off your emergency flares."

Captain Wilde shrugged. "Well then, he'll be in no doubt he needs to get here PDQ, won't he? Let's leave a token crew here to wait for him and guard your prisoners. The rest can sail with me and Pickle."

Reef frowned. "I'm not comfortable with this. I know Jasmine Peacock is missing and likely in some danger but, as the Commodore's representative here, I cannot agree to sending the rest of the Barracudas directly into the enemy zone."

"The Commodore's representative, eh? Is that what you are?" Captain Wilde was grinning. "Let's put this to the vote. All those in favour of sailing right now to Atafutura Atoll to rescue Jasmine, raise your right hand now."

Every Barracudas' right hand shot up to the sunset sky. On either side of Reef, the hands of Harper and Antoni were also raised.

"OK," Captain Wilde said. "Now, all those in favour of dawdling here on this beach until Commodore Kuo and Captain Salt finally arrive, please raise *your* right hand now."

All eyes turned to Reef as he alone raised his hand. His face was red – and this could not be blamed on the setting sun.

"That settles it!" Captain Wilde rubbed her hands together. "We set sail in five."

Captain Wilde turned to Reef. "You have the makings of a fine pirate." She put her hand on his cheek. "You just need to learn to bend the rules from time to time."

Blushing furiously, Reef just about managed to keep his composure. "I had better go and find a Fishtail to send an updated message to the Academy."

"If that makes you feel useful, do that," Captain Wilde said. "And then we'll agree which of you lot stays here to keep watch over the prisoners."

Everyone began racing across the sand, talking excitedly about their high-stakes mission.

"You!" Captain Wilde boomed, pointing a bony outstretched finger at Neo. Turning her hand over, she now made a crook of the finger to beckon him forwards. "I know you."

"Yes, you do." He smiled at her, watching the cogs spinning in her brain.

"You're Doll's boy! My, you've grown tall since last I clapped eyes on you, Ned Darkwater."

Neo reached out to tickle her little pig's chin. "It's been a while," he said. "These days, I go by the name Neo Splice."

Captain Wilde frowned. "Whyever would you do that? Ned Darkwater is a beautiful name."

Neo was surprised at the sudden rush of sadness he felt. Was this *ever* going to get easier?

"Been a while since I saw your lovely mother," December said now. "How is she doing?"

Neo found himself unable to answer the question with words. Instead, the Captain's face, the beach and the sea became a blur as tears splashed down his eyelashes. Before he knew it, Captain Wilde had folded him into a tight hug, one hand resting on his head. "There, there, Ned. It's all right, love. I can tell you and I have a bit of catching up to do."

CHAPTER 36
BEST SURPRISE EVER

Uncle Noah steered their boat through the shadow of a steep headland and Jasmine caught sight of a dramatically-shaped island up ahead. The weathered stone glowed golden in the light of the setting sun. This must be the atoll which Uncle Noah had spoken of. Jasmine felt her heart lift. Whatever her uncle's warped motives, he *was* taking her to see her mum.

Suddenly her excitement was pierced by fresh fears. If her mum was a prisoner of the League of True Pirates, then her dad must be too. There was no way of knowing how they had been treated these past weeks. She started to shiver at the thought of what might be waiting for her on the island. Were her parents held in a stark cell? How roughly had they been treated? Had they been deprived of food and water?

She found herself glaring at Noah, over at the wheel of the LOT P vessel. Perhaps he felt the weight of her stare because now he turned and smiled directly at her. He looked so relaxed, so in control. Jasmine wondered how long he had been planning all this. How long had he hated her parents – his own *sister* and her husband?

All this time, she had thought she had known Uncle Noah, but it turned out she hadn't known him at all.

***

As they made their final approach to the atoll, the boat hugged the low sea-cliffs on their port-side. Up ahead, the cliffs became even shorter. A narrow channel was revealed, which opened into a tranquil lagoon. As their boat sailed from the channel into the lagoon itself, Jasmine noticed that the surface of the water was as smooth as mirror glass, reflecting the dark pinks and fiery purples of the sunset sky.

As they sailed on, Jasmine counted several ships moored in the lagoon, their masts and sails casting dark pools of shadow over the still water. The ships looked, at first glance, like regular pirate ships. But, as they sailed closer, Jasmine noticed each had been painted black and now flew the ragged LOT P flag. Gazing up, she began to shiver again.

The lagoon encircled a small central island – an island within an island! Here, there were a few timber and iron buildings and more ships – which had not yet been fully converted. Jasmine realised this was some kind of shipyard. Although it was getting darker by the minute, people were still busy with work. She watched them moving back and forth between the ships and the shore, fetching paint and other supplies.

With a jolt, Jasmine noticed that none of the workers were dressed in the horrible uniform of LOT P agents she had met so far – the dark clothes, cloak and tell-tale figurehead mask. Instead, these workers here were dressed in more functional clothing, their faces unmasked. It made total sense. The sinister LOT P uniform was only necessary when you needed to strike fear into the hearts of those you met.

As Uncle Noah brought their boat into dock, Priya jumped down from the boat's bow onto the harbour and began tying up the lines. Cecile Binoche stepped effortlessly after her, helping to finish the job.

"Welcome to Atafutura Atoll," Priya told Jasmine, smiling at her from the dockside. "I think you'll find the work we are doing here . . . quite interesting."

Jasmine felt the fresh stab of Priya's betrayal. Biting down bitter words, she simply shook her head. She had no interest in the rotten work of the LOT P. All she wanted was to see her parents, to know they were safe and well. To hug them and have them hug her back.

Stepping away from the wheel, Noah turned around to address Jasmine. "You look worried, dear niece. Don't be. Trust me, this is going to be the best surprise ever." He smiled. "And, just to remind you, you are our guest here, *not* a prisoner."

Jasmine frowned, wondering again how far she could trust him. Following him onto the dock, she glanced around, trying to get a clearer sense of her surroundings. Her eyes ranged from the ships to the shipyard buildings, then to the people moving about on the harbour. She heard voices, including one extremely familiar one. A woman was giving instructions to a group of workers, gathered in front of one of the ships.

Jasmine broke away from Uncle Noah's side and ran along the dock. Moments later, her heart racing, Jasmine found herself face to face with the woman confidently giving instructions. The woman who she knew and loved better than anyone in the world.

Jasmine watched as her mum calmly told the others to go and finish their work. The crowd quickly dispersed. Now she was able to get a proper look at her mum, Jasmine's head was spinning.

Parker Ripley Peacock looked exceedingly well. She was dressed elegantly in a crisp black blouse, slim-fitting trousers and a pair of her favourite boots. She showed no sign of having been deprived of food or water. She seemed perfectly at home here, telling other people what to do. None of this was at all what Jasmine had been expecting.

Jasmine felt suddenly frozen to the spot. Her mother had now seen her, but she wasn't smiling. Parker twisted her black diamond wedding ring around her finger.

Uncle Noah arrived at Jasmine's side. He rested a hand on her shoulder, smiling broadly as he greeted his sister. "Look at the rare treasure I have brought you today."

Jasmine knew from her mother's expression that something was very, very wrong.

"What have you *done*, Noah?" Parker Ripley Peacock asked, her voice low and husky.

Uncle Noah nudged Jasmine forwards towards her mother. "Go on then, say hello!"

Hot tears prickled Jasmine's eyes. "Mum, it's so good to see you. You look so well . . ."

Jasmine ran out of words. Because it seemed super clear now that her mum wasn't a prisoner here at all. And, if Parker wasn't a prisoner of the League, then there was something worse, *much* worse, that Jasmine had not considered before.

As if reading her terrible thoughts, her mum's dark eyes met Jasmine's own. "My name is Parker Ripley Peacock," she said, her voice suddenly loud and full. "And I reject the rules of the Pirate Federation. Because I am, and always will be, a True Pirate."

"There!" Uncle Noah said, smiling and punching the air. "Just as I promised, Jasmine! Isn't this just the best surprise *ever*?"

CHAPTER 37
BRILLIANT DISGUISE

Jacoby felt fully back in the game! Sailing on board Captain Wilde's handsome junk, they had made excellent progress pursuing the LOT P boats to Atafutura Atoll.

December Wilde had done a tremendous job of keeping the LOT P flotilla – which included the four yachts stolen from the Barracudas – in her sights. Cloaked by the sunset sky, she had kept a safe distance so that the enemy would not rumble that they were being followed. As they made the final approach to the atoll, Captain Wilde gave the command for Reef and Shay to drop anchor. Captain Wilde strode over to Ocean, Pickle trotting along at her ankles.

"It's all on you and your crew from this point," Captain Wilde told Ocean. "Your boat has a much better chance of sailing unnoticed through the atoll and out again with your friend."

Ocean nodded. "We're ready," she said, eagerly. "Right, guys?"

Jacoby, Cosmo and Neo all gave Ocean a salute. "Yes, Captain!" they cried together.

"Touch Pickle for luck!" Captain Wilde scooped up her pet and held him towards them. They all obediently placed a hand on Pickle's plump body, then walked off towards the stern of *Brave as the Waves*, where the last remaining Academy yacht was tethered.

"Don't forget your totally brilliant disguise!" Fergus called out.

Jacoby raced back across the deck to collect from Fergus and Lewis the cloaks and masks they had taken from the two captured LOT P agents. Those agents were still held prisoner, back on the island, under the watchful eyes – and sharp swords – of Ari, Leif and Harper. Everyone else had travelled onwards on Captain Wilde's junk.

Jacoby dropped the cloaks and masks down into Neo's waiting hands, then climbed down to join his friends in the Academy yacht. They began sailing off down the narrow channel that would take them into Atafutura Atoll.

"We're coming for you, Jasmine!" Jacoby whispered.

Seated across from him, Neo nodded. "It's on."

***

Sailing silently towards the heart of the atoll, Ocean cleverly hugged the shadows both of the land mass itself and also the tall ships moored in the lagoon.

Jacoby's eyes were on stalks as they passed the splendid pirate ships that had been painted black and now flew the LOT P flag from their masts. He felt Neo's hand on his shoulder and, glancing up, saw that Neo was pointing ahead to where the flotilla had moored. The last of the LOT P agents who had stolen the Barracuda boats were now walking away from the dock, throwing their masks in the air and celebrating their success. Jacoby gritted his teeth, feeling even more determined to find Jasmine and pull her out of here. If that meant a bit of close combat with one or two agents of the League, *nessun problema*, as Captain Molina would say. After everything he'd endured in the past 24 hours, Jacoby had a few scores to settle.

Ocean found a spot close by the other Barracuda boats to moor her own. This seemed an excellent idea. There were already four Academy yachts here – one extra was unlikely to attract attention.

Jacoby's heart was racing. The success of the next

part of the mission rested on him and Neo. It was time to take their search onto the island itself!

The two brothers quickly fastened their cloaks around themselves and placed the stolen figurehead masks over their heads. Jacoby's nose wrinkled – his mask smelled a bit sweaty. The four young Barracudas gripped their hands together, then Jacoby and Neo stepped over onto the dock. Cosmo passed a sword up to each of his comrades. Just at the moment that Jacoby took his sword, a shaft of moonlight shone directly onto the scar of Calabria on Cosmo's face. Jacoby thought of Cosmo's noble ancestry. Then he thought of all the pirates who had come before them and fought brave battles to save their comrades. As he took hold of the sword, he knew what he had to do.

Swords in hand, Jacoby and Neo trod carefully along the jetty, moving in the direction of the cluster of warehouses and other shipyard buildings. Throughout, neither said a word. Glancing across at Neo, disguised in the spooky figurehead mask, Jacoby shuddered. He hoped he looked just as sinister. Behind the mask, he was beaming widely. There was no one he'd rather be on this mission with than his brother.

He caught Neo pointing and quickly understood

he was suggesting they take a short cut through the shadowy gap between two of the shipyard buildings. Instantly, Jacoby fell into step. He could hear muffled voices in the building to their starboard side.

They were almost at the end of the path between the buildings. Neo pointed again to signal they should turn left at the end. Jacoby nodded, still listening hard for any clue. But, before they had the chance to turn, someone stepped silently out into the path in front of them. She was holding an oil-lamp in one hand and a sword in the other. And, to Jacoby's horror, he *knew* her.

It was Priyanka Swift.

"Hold up!" Priya called out.

Jacoby and Neo froze.

"Why are you both masked?" Priya asked. "You know it's against the rules to wear masks here on the island."

There was an awkward silence. Jacoby decided to take control. Clearing his throat, he put on a deep, rough voice. "We just docked the last of the boats we stole from those dumb Academy kids," he said. "We'll change out of this gear in a jiffy."

Priya's nose wrinkled, as if she was picking up an unpleasant smell. "I think you should probably remove your masks right now," she said.

Jacoby made his voice even deeper and rougher. "And I think you can mind your own business! You're only the newbie recruit here. You don't get to call the shots." He was enjoying this. If he said so himself, he might have the makings of a rather good spy.

Priya shook her head, set down her lamp and, raising her sword, sprang into attack position.

"Jacoby Blunt," she said. "I already guessed it was you before you used the very same voice you did in the Christmas production of *Pirates of Penzance* last year."

Jacoby's shoulders slumped. She was right! Perhaps his spy routine needed a little fine tuning.

He threw off his mask. Neo did the same. They raised their swords at the exact same moment. But Priya did not look scared – which was more than a bit worrying. Because Priyanka Swift was well known for always having one more trick up her sleeve.

CHAPTER 38
TRUTH AND SPIES

"We can talk privately in here," Parker told Jasmine, twisting open the door into one of the timber and iron shipyard buildings. It had been split into two spaces – a small office at the front and an open warehouse at the back. The warehouse was big enough to house a ship and, indeed, a full-size pirate galleon was visible through the glass wall that separated the office from the warehouse.

Jasmine followed her mum into the office, feeling every nerve in her body in shreds at her mother's declaration out on the dock. In the centre of the room was a desk with a captain's swivel chair. The desk's surface was covered with books and papers – ships' ledgers, maps, cross-sections. Jasmine spied notes in her mother's neat handwriting on every document. It was clear this desk belonged to Parker Ripley Peacock, even before she sat down in the captain's chair and pointed for Jasmine to take a seat opposite.

"Here's a glass of water," her mum said. "Sip it slowly. It will help with the shock."

As Jasmine drank, she stared past Parker at the wall behind the desk. This was covered with paper too. There were pins keeping everything in place and lines of coloured string connecting the pins. Parker Ripley Peacock had always been a dedicated planner.

Her mum cleared some papers from the centre of the desk and, folding her arms, leant towards Jasmine. "Well, my darling, I'm sure you have a few questions for me," she said.

Jasmine almost choked on her mouthful of water. She set the glass down carefully. She was no longer trembling but could now feel something like an electric current pulsing through her. When she spoke, she was surprised to hear her voice sounded quite calm.

"Please tell me you are a spy, Mum. That you are working undercover for the Pirate Federation and *that's* why you are here, cleverly *pretending* to be an agent of the League."

Her mother leant back in her chair, running a hand through her sleek, dark hair, as she considered the question. Then she turned back to meet Jasmine's gaze.

"A spy? Is that really what you think?" She shook her head. "No, I'm not a Federation spy. I am, in fact, one of the founding pirates of the League." She sounded proud and excited. Jasmine felt sick.

"I know this will take time to absorb and, just to be clear, this is *not* how I was planning to tell you. But, true to form, your uncle got an itch he had to scratch." Her lovely smile was like the sun coming out from behind storm clouds. "Putting that aside, it truly is wonderful to see you, my darling."

Jasmine's stomach clenched in knots. Could she trust her mother's smile now? Parker Ripley Peacock calmly took a sip of water. "Well," she said, "there's no need to rush things. We're going to be here a few days before moving on." It seemed already decided that Jasmine would be staying with her. "Plenty of time for a mum-and-daughter catch-up."

"Is Dad here too?" Jasmine interrupted her. Suddenly, it felt vitally important to know where Captain Jonathan Peacock stood in all this horror.

"Your father's off at another of our bases," Parker said. "That's where I'm heading later in the week." She tapped the desktop. "We will sail there together, you and I."

Jasmine felt a hot, tearing sensation in her chest. Was this how it felt for a heart to break?

"So Dad is part of the League of True Pirates too?" Why, Jasmine wondered, did her mouth keep asking questions her ears didn't want the answers to?

Parker nodded. "Of course." She smiled, happily. "He's going to be so thrilled to see you – we've both missed you terribly all these weeks, but we've had so much to prepare in such a short amount of time. You do understand?" She twisted her wedding ring again.

There was nothing about this conversation that made any kind of sense to Jasmine. It was as if her wonderful, smart, kind, beautiful mother had been body-snatched by an alien life-form. This woman *looked* like her mum, *sounded* liked her mum, wore her mum's smart clothes and lovely gardenia perfume. But this *wasn't* her mum. It couldn't be.

"Are you absolutely sure you're not a spy? Both you and Dad?" Jasmine's voice was hoarse.

Parker frowned. "I am quite sure and, frankly, it's going to get tired very quickly if you keep asking that. You need to understand this is how change so often happens in the world we live in. It can be extremely sudden, tremendously exciting, mildly disorientating, perhaps . . . but you have to hold tight and grip onto it like a wave that's guiding you to your glorious future."

Jasmine shook her head, her eyes slick with tears. "Why did you send me your music box – with the coded message?" she asked now. "Assuming it *was* you who sent it?"

"Of course it was!" Her mother's dark eyes flashed fire as she rose from her seat. "I sent you the box and the message so you wouldn't worry, and would know we were safe."

Jasmine blotted her eyes. The music box had not only told her that her parents were safe. It had also made *her* feel safe – for a while. Now, everything had changed. She wasn't sure she would ever feel safe again.

There was a drumming knock at the office door. "Enter!" her mum called out.

A man appeared in the doorway. "Sorry to interrupt, Commodore Peacock, but you are urgently needed in Dock 3."

"Not a problem," Parker said, glancing across at Jasmine. "This won't take long. Sit tight, my darling. We'll pick this up shortly."

"He called you *Commodore Peacock*!" Jasmine said, reeling with fresh shock.

Her mum smiled, already halfway through the door. "Your mother is one of the top people here. You should be very proud."

The door now closed between them. Still, Jasmine heard her mother inform the man, "I can make my own way down to Dock 3, Lieutenant Hutton. Please wait here and make sure my daughter doesn't do anything rash. Any dramas, you know what to do."

The man quickly agreed to her mother's command. Jasmine shook her head. It seemed she was now her own mother's prisoner.

She decided to take advantage of Parker's absence – however short – to take a look at some of the documents pinned to the wall. There were plans of ships, crew lists, tidal charts and maps with a lot of stars, circles and notes inked on them. Clearly these pieces all added up to a big plan, but it was impossible for Jasmine to put it all together when she was so tired and reeling in shock. She reached out a hand to smooth down the corner of one of the maps. As she did, there were three sharp taps on the glass wall opposite.

Turning, she was shocked to see Priya standing on the other side of the glass. The index finger of one hand

was pressed tight against Priya's lips. The other was beckoning to her.

Rooted to the spot, Jasmine watched as the door in the centre of the wall gently opened. Priya now turned from Jasmine and began walking away into the back section of the warehouse. Jasmine stared in disbelief at the open doorway.

Was this another trick? Or was it possible that Priya – Priya, of all people! – was offering her an escape route?

CHAPTER 39
PRIYA'S GIFT

Deciding to trust her gut, Jasmine took a deep breath, slipped through the doorway and followed her former classmate into the shadowy depths of the warehouse. As she stepped through to the other side, she realised that the warehouse was in fact a vast dry dock with a deep well, which was how a full-sized pirate galleon came to be resting there. On the near side of the dock was scaffolding with a metal stairwell bolted onto it. Priya was waiting for Jasmine at the top of the stairs, with a lantern in her hand and an impatient expression on her face.

The further she ran on, the darker it grew. Jasmine was aware of the perilous drop down from this level to the base of the dry dock many metres below. Glancing back at the ship, her heart skipped a beat. There, at eye level, was the ship's name, painted in ornate azure and gold letters. *The Blue Marlin*. There was the beautiful painting of a fish jumping out of the ocean, now surrounded by dull black paint. So this was to be the next ship converted into a LOT P vessel. A day ago, the sight of it would have totally floored Jasmine. Now, she felt only a numb sense of sadness.

"Come on," Priya hissed. "There isn't much time."

Arriving at last at Priya's side, Jasmine said, "Tell me why I should trust you."

Priya didn't miss a beat. "One, because you're the smartest kid in Barracuda class, present company excluded. Two, you have amazing gut instincts." Priya nodded. "Now, you need to listen fast and then, if you agree, move faster. Down there! Understand?"

Jasmine glanced down and found herself reeling at the empty drop between the bars of the scaffolding. "I understand," she said, her voice wobbly.

"You know now that your mum is one of the ringleaders of the League," Priya said. "It sucks, I know, but you'll adjust."

"That's what she said too—"

Priya forged on. "The good news is your dad is not part of this. He's working undercover to start the fightback."

"But she said—"

"She's lying," Priya said. "I'm sorry, Jasmine. I know this is hard. You can't trust your mum. But you can trust me. I am *not* an agent of the League. What you saw on *Academy Alpha* was all staged. I've been preparing for this for months."

Jasmine's head was buzzing with questions, but Priya continued before she could cut in. "I'm undercover, here," Priya told her. "And I'm making it my business to get you safely off this island, *if* that's what you want. The crisis I created in Dock 3 is only going to distract your mother for so long."

"You created a crisis . . . to *help* me?"

Priya nodded. "Time to decide, Jasmine. Stay or go."

Jasmine felt a tearing pain in her head. "I could stay . . . I could go undercover too . . . make my mum think I'm fully on board, but . . ." Her words faltered as Priya shook her head sharply.

"You're not me, Jasmine," Priya told her. "Your face is an open book. Don't beat yourself up about it. You have plenty of qualities I don't have. And I have undergone rigorous training by Commodore Kuo and the Feds for the past eighteen months."

Jasmine was stunned by this. "They've been training you since . . . you were *nine years old*?"

Priya nodded with justifiable pride. "They singled me out in Crab Class."

"But," Jasmine frowned, "LOT P hasn't been going that long, has it?"

"The timeline is hazy," Priya explained. "I was the Federation's experiment. They trained me to be a secret weapon ready for any threat to their power. So when the time came . . ."

"You were ready!"

"Exactly." Priya frowned again. "I'm sorry, Jasmine, but now you have to decide. Stay or go. If we delay any further, I risk blowing my cover. And I can't do that, not even for you."

Suddenly Jasmine felt the answer in every atom pulsing in her body. "Get me out of here!"

Without wasting another second, Priya stepped across onto the scaffolding and held out the lantern to light Jasmine's way. Jasmine took a couple of steadying breaths, then stepped after Priya onto the top of the metal stairwell.

They made their descent at lighting speed. There was no time to talk and Jasmine needed to put her full attention on where she was placing her feet in order to avoid falling into the void. It felt as if she held her breath throughout the entire descent down the six flights of metal stairs, but she knew that couldn't have been the case. As she stepped foot onto solid ground at the base of the dry dock, she realised her body was trembling wildly and her legs were now as wobbly as jelly. Still, there was no time to rest. Priya had run on ahead to a door, which she now tore open, beckoning Jasmine onwards again.

Horrible thoughts crossed Jasmine's mind. *What if this is all a trick? What if Priya isn't the Federation's secret weapon but a true agent of the League? What if she's luring me into a dungeon prison or another vile trap?* But Priya had been dead right before. Jasmine *did* have amazing gut instincts. And they were telling her that Priya was her ally not her enemy. Her enemy, heart-breaking though it was to admit, was her own mother.

Jasmine ran on after Priya and found herself inside a tunnel. "Not another tunnel!" she cried out, letting her voice release some of the anger that had been building inside her.

Priya laughed. "Only a short one, this time, I promise."

She was good to her word because, barely a minute

later, Jasmine felt the fresh kiss of night air and found herself standing alongside Priya at the edge of the lagoon. And there, waiting for her in an Academy yacht, were Ocean and Cosmo, Jacoby and Neo. At the sheer relief of seeing her friends, Jasmine's legs began to buckle. Priya caught her before she fell and, supporting her all the way, led her over to the boat and her friends.

Jacoby and Neo reached out their arms for Jasmine and eased her safely into the boat.

"Thank you!" she told Priya but found Priya was already running off to cover her tracks. Ever the efficient agent. It was only as Jasmine sat up and smiled at her friends that she realised there was a folded piece of paper in her hands. Priya must have placed it there. Jasmine closed her fist tightly over Priya's gift. Whatever this was, it could wait.

"It's so good to see you," Jacoby told her. "I was *beyond* worried."

"You too!" Jasmine said. "And your bite is back under control!" She glanced over at Neo. "You found him the anti-venom."

"*We* did!" Neo said, with a broad grin, looping an arm around Cosmo's shoulder.

"Ready to leave this abomination of an atoll?" Ocean asked now, hand on the wheel.

There could only be one response to that. It came from four weary but undefeated voices. "Yes, Captain!"

CHAPTER 40
JOURNEYS

The Academy yacht, captained by Ocean, sailed towards Captain Wilde's ship, which was moored safely beyond the outer reaches of Atafutura Atoll. There were cheers from the Barracudas lined up along the deck rail of *Brave as the Waves.* Jacoby beamed to see Wing and Fergus, Layla and Shay and all his other young friends jumping up and down and cheering. Everyone was thrilled at the success of the rescue mission.

Jacoby looked around the yacht and saw his crewmates were smiling too. All except Jasmine. She looked utterly drained. Like the others, Jacoby had been shocked to the core when Jasmine informed them her mum was one of the ringleaders of the League of True Pirates. Jacoby couldn't imagine how he'd feel if he found out that his mum or dad were involved in LOT P. Or rather, he *could* imagine. It would be horrible.

Cosmo and Neo tethered the boat to Captain Wilde's

ship and the five weary but triumphant pirate apprentices climbed up onto deck, met with fist-bumps, high-fives and hugs from their classmates. For a moment, Jasmine was lost in the crowd.

"Excellent job!" Captain Wilde told Ocean. "Knew you'd make a success of it!"

Ocean smiled, modestly. "It helped that I had a pretty awesome crew."

You're not wrong, thought Jacoby, throwing his arms happily around Neo and Cosmo.

Reef Lermentov strode past the captain towards his sister. "I'm so proud of you, Ocean," he said, folding her into a hug. She seemed surprised but also delighted.

Some of the Barracudas were now shouting excitedly and pointing out to sea, having spotted another ship sailing towards them. They recognised the shape of *Academy Alpha*, one of Pirate Academy's three school galleons, cresting the waves. As it came closer, they saw Commodore Kuo and Captain Salt at the bow, waving. There were fresh cheers.

Oceans Bound weekend was officially at an end. It was time to return to Pirate Academy.

"I see your Fishtail successfully messaged the Commodore," December Wilde told Reef. He nodded.

"Good job, Reef Lermentov," she told him. "I suppose we'll be saying our goodbyes shortly, but I shall look forward to joining forces with you again sometime."

"Thank you," Reef said, smiling. "I've learnt so much from you."

***

Once *Academy Alpha* pulled up alongside *Brave as the Waves*, arrangements were swiftly made for the Academy students to move decks for the homeward journey. Jacoby and Neo were tasked with untethering the last remaining yacht from *Brave as the Waves* and attaching it to the main Academy ship.

"I couldn't have done any of this without you," Jacoby told Neo, inside the small yacht.

"That cuts both ways," Neo said. "We're a great team. Splice and Blunt."

Jacoby grinned. "*Yes*, but I think what you mean to say is . . . Blunt and Splice."

The brothers' eyes met. Blue-green. Green-blue. Just like the water lapping their small boat.

***

As December Wilde's ship sailed away into the night, the Commodore, Captain Salt, Captain Platonov, Captain Singh and Captain Larsen all welcomed the students back onto *Academy Alpha*. The ship first sailed over to the island to collect Ari, Leif and Harper and the two LOT P agents the Barracudas had captured there. "You've made me incredibly proud today," Captain Larsen told her son, ruffling his hair fondly.

"Mor!" he protested. "Not in front of the prisoners!"

Once the LOT P agents were safely secured in the vaults of *Academy Alpha* – under the armed guard of three Academy Captains – the ship sailed on to its final destination. On the main deck, the Barracudas gathered together, in front of a beaming Commodore Kuo and Captain Salt.

"This isn't the time for a big speech," the headcaptain began, prompting a smile from his deputy. "From everything we hear, this has been a highly unusual Oceans Bound weekend, and we are looking forward to a detailed debrief from you over the next day or two. For now, Captain Salt and I just want you to know how proud we are of each and every one of you Barracudas." He paused. "Truly, you have proved yourselves to be exceptional young pirates, demonstrating every one of the key talents we ask of you. I know you will have learnt so much from the challenges you faced this weekend . . . both the official challenges and the unexpected ones.

I believe you are returning to Pirate Academy as an even stronger, more invincible crew than ever." Jacoby smiled to himself, wondering if the Commodore had noticed someone was missing.

Once the headcaptain's speech was over, the Barracudas began clustering around Jasmine again, bombarding her with well-meaning, but tiring, questions.

Jacoby cleared his throat. "That's enough for now," he said, firmly. "Jasmine needs time to rest after everything she has been through." No one objected and Jacoby reached out his hand and led his friend over to a quiet spot at the front of *Academy Alpha*. They found a seat for themselves directly under the foresail.

"Thank you," Jasmine told him. "This is just what I need."

"I know . . ." He quickly corrected himself. "I mean, I'm *glad*." They sat in silence for a while.

"Jasmine," Jacoby asked. "When you came back on board the yacht, I thought I saw you looking at a piece of paper. I just wondered, was it anything . . . interesting?"

Smiling, Jasmine reached into her pocket, then passed the folded square over to her friend.

"This might help you find your dad," Jacoby read aloud, his eyes wide. "Good luck!"

"Priya gave it to me," Jasmine explained. "You can open it, if you like."

Jacoby sighed. "I still can't believe Priya *isn't* working for LOT P . . . She's one of the good guys!"

As Jasmine's face fell, Jacoby reddened. "I'm sorry," he said. "I think I'd better just shut up!"

Jasmine shook her head, smiling kindly. "It's OK," she said. "Just give me a little time."

He nodded. "Take all the time you need."

Jasmine relaxed back into her seat, then suddenly bolted upright and started scanning the deck. "Jacoby," she said, sounding worried. "I haven't seen Neo in a while."

Jacoby nodded. "You'd have to have truly amazing eyesight to see him right now."

"What do you mean?" she asked. "Is everything OK?"

Jacoby nodded. "Everything's fine. But it might be a little while before we see him again."

Now Jasmine was fully alert. "Jacoby, you're starting to scare me."

He shook his head. "Don't be scared! Remember the co-ordinates he found – the ones from the bracelet his mum gave him? Well, he decided it was time to find out where they lead."

"He has? But how?" Jasmine's dark eyes were wide.

"And, Jacoby, didn't you want to go with him to help? You are brothers, after all."

Jacoby nodded. "Yes, we are. Neo did ask if I'd like to go with. And of course I was tempted. But I told him no – it's more important for me to stay and look after *my sister*."

Jasmine's eyes narrowed. "You mean . . . but I'm not . . ."

Jacoby took her hand and squeezed it. "As good as," he said.

Jasmine shook her head. "You really are extraordinary, Jacoby Blunt," she said.

Her words brought a lump to Jacoby's throat. "Not yet," he said. "But I'm working on it."

***

Neo stood by the ship's wheel, cradling Pickle in his arms, as December Wilde steered them boldly on by the light of the stars and moon.

"Won't you miss your friends while we are gone?" the captain asked him.

Neo stroked Pickle's chin. "I will miss them," he said. But it was more of a happy thought than a sad one because he realised that, in the past few weeks, he had made the best friends in his life so far. Not to mention his beloved-if-fairly-bonkers brother. "But I *have* to do this. And I'm so grateful to you for helping me."

Captain Wilde shook her head. "It's a pleasure to help you," she said. "And to do something for our dear, departed Doll. Besides, I see now that my brain cells were wasting away in that sleepy backwater. Every bone in my body is ready for a whole new adventure."

Pickle had started to wriggle and Neo crouched down to let him potter freely around the deck. "I wonder just how long we'll be gone," Neo said, standing up again.

December adjusted the wheel very slightly. "Who can say?" she shrugged. "But, as someone wise once told me, sometimes you just have to trust the tide. Think you can do that?"

Neo's blue-green eyes were wide as he took in the vast expanse of ocean and sky spread out before him. The world was so big and so beautiful, so full of mystery and wonder. As *Brave as the Waves* coursed on through the night, Neo stretched out his arms and felt new energy pulsing through his body from his fingertips to his toes.

"Yes," he cried out. "Yes, Captain Wilde. I think I can."

TO BE CONTINUED ...

PIRATE ACADEMY:
WHOSE SHIP IS WHOSE?

Now you have read the first two PIRATE ACADEMY adventures, you've encountered quite a few ships, belonging to the Barracudas' pirating parents and other famous pirates – so let's see if you can remember whose ship is whose!

Below is a list of ship names and a list of famous pirate captains. Your task is to match the ship to its captain(s). Answers are at the foot of the page.

THE SHIPS	THE CAPTAINS
1. Death and the Maiden	A. December Wilde
2. The Blue Marlin	B. Clothilde and Beaufort Blunt (Jacoby's parents)
3. Academy Alpha	C. Cressida Moon (one of Wing's mums)
4. The Enigma	D. Parker Ripley Peacock and Jonathan Peacock (Jasmine's parents)
5. The Orcadian	E. Eriska and Unst Fairbrossen (parents of Fergus and Lewis)
6. The North Star	F. Doll Darkwater (Neo's mum)
7. The Conundrum	G. Raven Moon (one of Wing's mums)
8. Brave as the Waves	H. One of the three galleons belonging to the Pirate Academy fleet

Now, imagine that you are a student in
Barracuda Class and have a famous pirate family!
What would your ship be called?

Maybe you feel inspired to draw the ship's flag or
even the entire ship. Justin Somper would love to see
what you come up with, so why not ask your parent or
teacher to share your art with him on Instagram?
You can find him @JustinSomper.

You never know . . . you might find YOUR ship name
features in a future PIRATE ACADEMY book!

THANK YOUS

Although my name is on the front cover, this book wouldn't be in your hands were it not for a sizeable crew working away behind the scenes. Let me introduce you to some of them...

Firstly, Hazel Holmes, Publisher at UCLan – thanks so much for embarking on this fresh adventure with me and for giving Pirate Academy (and Vampirates) so much care, attention and support. Thanks to Antonia Wilkinson for the stellar PR campaign that launched the new series so strongly, and to Charlotte Rothwell and Graeme Williams for your awesome work on the marketing front. Thanks to the incomparable Phil Perry for your PR support.

After many years of waiting (not so patiently), I finally got to work with my dream editor. Anne McNeil, thank you for coming on board and giving so much of your time, wisdom and passion to this project. You have made me a better writer and done so much to build my confidence. So excited to sail forward on this series, and other new work, with you.

Jasmine Dove, I feel so lucky to have you as my copy editor. Your detailed reading of the text and nuanced understanding of the characters is so appreciated. I trust you completely and know the books will always be better after your deep dive into them.

Jake Hope – you're not just one of the world's leading youth librarians but one of the most generous humans. You have been one of the very first readers of each of the Pirate Academy books and I'm so grateful for your kind and thoughtful feedback. Thanks for making time for this between your many other commitments.

Amy Cooper, you made the Vampirates books look so beautiful and now you've done it again with Pirate Academy. Thanks for all the inspired, thoughtful and detailed work you put into our collaboration. And thanks too for recruiting the legend that is Teo Skaffa.

Captain Skaffa, it's just brilliant to have you on board for Pirate Academy. Thanks for giving my characters and story-world such a strong visual identity and for all the energy, love and sheer fun you bring to this project. I couldn't have asked for a better partner-in-piracy!

Thank you to Robert Snuggs and your wonderful crew at Bounce Sales & Marketing for all your dedicated work getting my books into bookshops throughout the UK and Ireland.

Huge thanks to my formidable crew of agents at Curtis Brown – Stephanie Thwaites, Izzy Gahan, Roxane Edouard, Grace Robinson, Savanna Wicks, Enrichetta Frezzato, Anna Weguelin, Theo Roberts and Jazz Adamson. Thanks also to Gwen Beal at UTA.

There's a hashtag on Instagram - #authorssupportingauthors – and it's indicative of what a generous industry we work in where fellow authors are willing to pause their own writing, editing and other commitments to take a look at your new writing. I am so grateful to my fellow writers and creators who took time out to have an early read of Pirate Academy. Thank you Guy Bass, Janine Beacham, Jennifer Bell, Chris Bradford, Eoin Colfer, Cressida Cowell, Laura Dockrill, Abi Elphinstone, Viv French, Chris Smith and Mel Taylor-Bessent.

The same goes for all those teachers, reading and education experts who gave Pirate Academy an early read and shared feedback online. These include Dean Boddington (No Shelf Control), Nicki Cleveland (Miss Cleveland Reads), Jane Etheridge (Federation of Children's Book Groups), Tom Griffiths (Check 'em Out Books), Erin Hamilton (FCBG/My Shelves are Full), Bev Humphrey (School Library Association/@LibWithAttitude), Jake Metselaar (@JakesBooks), Veronica Price (V's View from the Bookshelves), Jim Sells (National Literacy Trust), Emma Suffield (Little Blog of Library Treasures), Jacqui Sydney (Mrs Sydney's Famous World's Smallest Library), Danni Williams (For Books Sake) and Sue Wilsher (Through the Bookshelf). Thanks to you all not only for supporting Pirate Academy but for everything you do to support and nurture children's reading in the UK. Special thanks to Scott Evans (aka The Reading Teacher/@mreprimary) for co-creating our awesome Education Pack.

As you know, one of the main characters in Barracuda Class – Leif Larsen – has limb difference. I am extremely grateful to the support and advice received from Carly Bauert at LimbPower (limbpower. com) and Wendy McCleave at the Douglas Bader Foundation (douglasbaderfoundation.com). Thank you both for being so receptive to Leif, for helping me to represent him accurately and for welcoming me into your community.

As ever, I have had tireless support from my family whilst creating Pirate Academy. Thanks to my sister Jenny Jenner who is always one of my first readers and arguably my biggest champion. Thanks to Emma Somper & Jack Gearing for kindly flying out to Perth to celebrate publication day with me! A massive thanks to my great (in every sense) nephew, Henry Dewhirst, who dressed up (brilliantly) as Jacoby for World Book Day 2024, which also happened to be publication day of PIRATE ACADEMY: NEW KID ON DECK.

I've had wonderful support from friends, in and out of the publishing world – thank you Ros Bartlett, Peter Berry, Helen Boyle, Alice Burden, Mary Byrne, Nicole ("Nurse") Carmichael, Carla Gottgens, Natasha Harding, Caroline Horn, Jacqui Jones, Oliver Wilmot Jones, Damian Kelleher, Serena Lacey, (Karma is . . .) Kat McKenna, Anita Naik, Sarah Stuffins, Helen Varley, Ewan Vinnicombe, Sarah Webb, Penny Webber and Jo Williams. Special mention to Tony Wilmot – YOU know why – and to Tom O'Neill for the uplifting morning chats.

As always, the biggest thank you goes to my better half, Phil "PJ" Norman - also known as @authorprofile – who has beautifully designed so many key elements of Pirate Academy, from Instagram tiles to the Kids' Activity Pack. When there is film footage of me at the coast, it's PJ behind the camera, often with a towel over his head! He's also a one man "writers' room" who knows when we need an end-of-day walk to hammer out a fresh twist in the story. Beyond all this, PJ is my rock. He continues to spur me on to new heights and I have him to thank for encouraging me to finally take an idea I'd been harbouring for a long time to transform Pirate Academy into its very own series. PJ has consistently encouraged me to put my writing front-and-centre and believe in myself – for which I am deeply grateful.

Justin Somper

Download our FREE

Pirate Academy: Kids' Activity Pack

Pirate Academy: Education Resources

from uclanpublishing.com

Jasmine, Jacoby and Neo
will return in . . .

PIRATE ACADEMY

BOOK THREE:
SWORD ECHOES

PUBLISHING 2025